LOWCOUNTRY LEGENDS

T.K. RICHARDS

ALANA KIRKWOOD

DEDICATION

To Torris L. Henry, the real legend of my family. Your all-star status was stolen from the world too soon. We miss you dearly, and will forever love you. Gone but never forgotten.

Note from the Author

This book is a work of fiction and contains magical themes, stories of historic roots lived in the southern hemisphere of The United States, Geechee/Gullah dialect for example: whatchu is said in place of what did you, I'ne know is said in place of I don't know. Another way we say I don't or I ain't is I'on (pronounced ah-ow-on). Trying to= tryna. Children=churn and chirren. That=dat. Innit=a colloquial way to confirm you are believed, or you agree (chopped up from isn't it in most cases). These are just a few you will read in this story.

This book contains mentions of drug use, gun use, fear, local folklore, mythical beings, and adultery.

Connect with me on my website, or by signing up for my newsletter here:
https://www.tkrichards.com
https://tkrichardsnewsletter.ck.page
Follow me on Amazon for easy access to all of my work below:
https://www.amazon.com/author/tkrichards

"The South Got Somethin' To Say"
Andre 3000

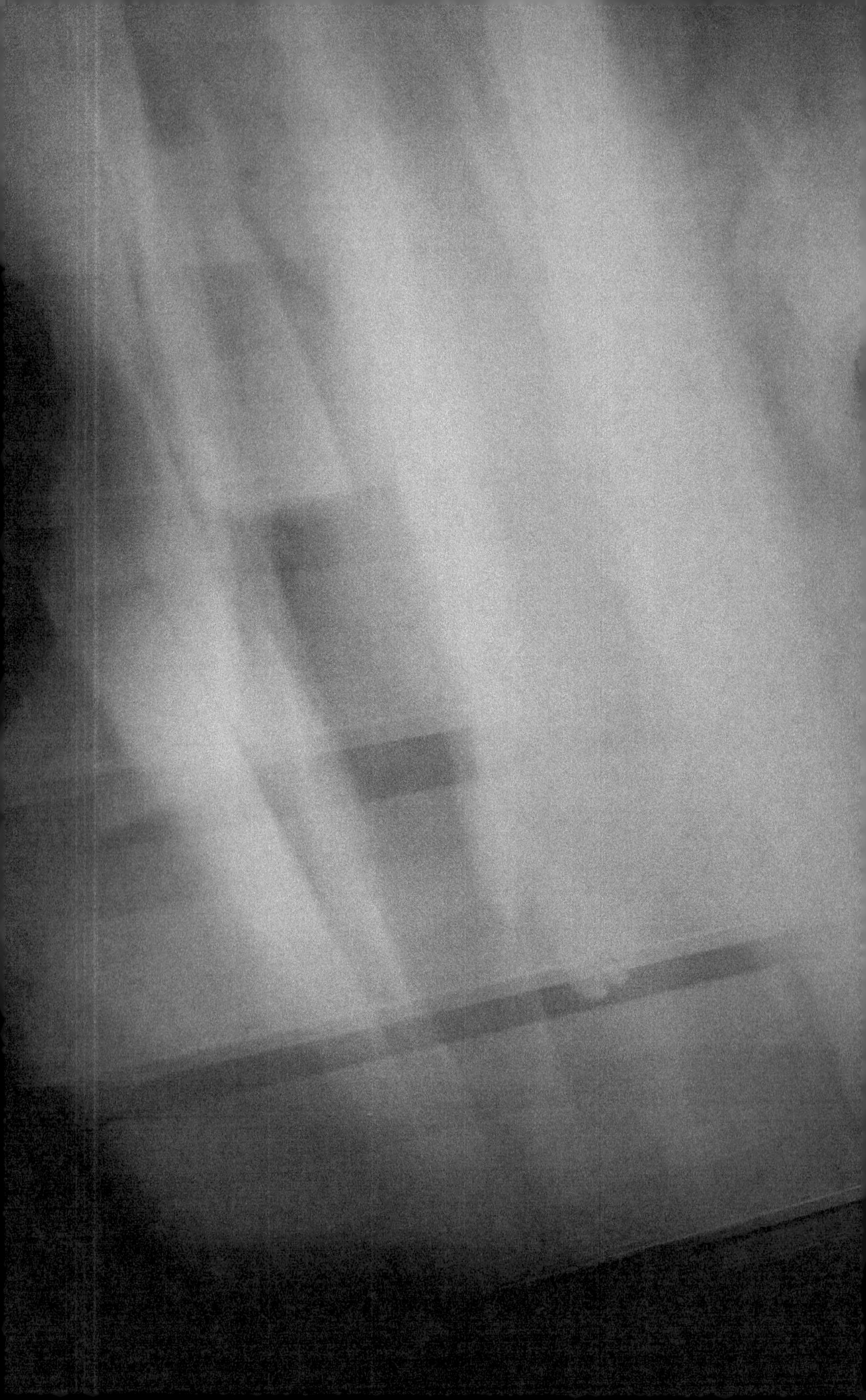

CHAPTER 1

VANYA'S VISION

The walk up the hill to Gran's house in ninety degree heat feels like punishment. My envelope pushing sister, Tamara, wipes her forehead with her sleeve.

"Gran has never made us wait outside before. She's normally home on the days we have to come here."

I run up the stairs and bang on the door. "She is here." I sit on the top step to rest and wait for her to open the door. "I saw her standing in the window when the bus pulled up."

"You just can't be wrong. Can you, Van?" Tamara lowers the strap on her book bag and sits on the step below me. "Her car isn't in the driveway, genius."

"I know what I saw. Just give her a minute. She'll let us in."

Tamara pulls out a joint from the side of her book bag. "Here. Smoke this. You need it more than I do." She taps the side of my face with it and laughs.

I push her hand away from my face. "What is that supposed to mean?"

"It means you need to relax. Always claiming you see things."

Tamara sparks a fire from the stolen pack of matches she swiped from Granddad's room.

"I do see things. And I saw her silhouette standing through the glass. I swear." My nostrils flare then scrunch when I rush through the cloud of smoke. "You know she's gonna smell that on you, right?"

"I'll be high by the time she gets here. I won't care." She inhales a second toke.

I pull out a folder from my bag, then spread it wide on top of the hood of the broken-down truck in the yard. I sit on the stacks of paper to protect my butt from heat rash, and finish up the last of my homework. Clouds show us mercy and briefly hide the sun beaming down on us. It's the first break we get since getting off the hot bus with the broken air conditioner that dropped us off at the end of the road.

"Thank God," I say, fanning myself with my notebook. "You know we wouldn't have to wait outside if you didn't steal Granddad's watch." I roll my eyes. "I'm always paying the price for your fuck-ups."

"Goody two-shoes," Tamara mutters under her breath.

I peer over at her. "*Whatchu* say?"

Tamara spits obscenities and threats of what she'll do to me if I find the courage to repeat my question in her face.

She warns. "If you're feeling froggy, then jump, Sis."

I sit bug-eyed, quiet, and still, staring at the woman peeking through the window behind Tamara.

She continues to bait me. "I didn't think you had the balls to come over here." She blows smoke from the side of her mouth as if she's been smoking for years. "And what the hell are you looking at?"

I swallow a big gulp of air. I'm too stunned to speak. Too afraid to take my eyes off of the woman I saw in the window when the bus dropped us off.

I blink and she's still there. Tamara badgers me, but I know if I speak she'll vanish like before and make me out to be a liar.

Tamara asks again, "Hey freakshow. What are you staring at?"

Because I don't answer, she pulls out her phone to take a selfie. "Holy shit!" She jumps up and runs next to me on the truck. The apparition vanishes. "I saw her that time." Her voice shakes. "That wasn't Gran."

"I know."

"Where the fuck did it go!" Tamara yells, enlarging the photo on the screen. "She looks a little like Gran though. Except…"

"Let me see that." I snatch her phone.

"Think I'm the first person to catch something like this in a photo?"

"I seriously doubt that."

The crunching sound of rocks being crushed by tires creep behind us.

"Gran's finally home." I pass the phone back to Tamara. "You show her."

She runs over to the car. Gran scowls at her standing in the way of her parking spot and fans her hands for Tamara to get out of the way. She lowers the window while the car is still rolling.

"What is it, chile?"

Tamara leans in her window once the car is parked. "Look what I caught on camera. A ghost is in your house."

Gran looks at the picture and scoffs. "Help me with the groceries."

"You don't seem shocked," says Tamara.

"Or scared," I add.

"Why would I be scared of my great-grandmother?"

Tamara's eyes bulge as she gasps softly. Her shuddering hands put the bag of groceries she'd picked up back down on the seat.

"I'm not going in there. I'll wait out here until Ma picks us up."

"Hush up chile and bring in my ice cream before it melts. Smelling like that *reefer*. It's ninety-something degrees out here."

I shrug my shoulders and hop off the truck. "I *don't* guess it will hurt us since we're family."

Tamara is glued to my heels when we enter the house, looking over her shoulders wide-eyed and pale. Gran goes about her business and gets dinner started. I sit at the kitchen table and complete our homework in the one class we share, and the one class Tamara needs to pull up her grade.

Gran stirs her rue. "Tam, don't you have homework, too?"

"Yes ma'am. I'm just...I'm just..." Tamara stammers.

"Waiting on your sister to finish so you can copy. You know my great-grandmother was a school teacher. You're probably the reason she showed up. She must be trying to tell you something. Most people don't catch such images with their camera. You must be touched."

Tamara's voice trembles. "I don't *wanna* be touched. I don't *wanna* see anything like that ever again."

I sneak my fork under the table and poke Tamara in the knee.

"Ah!" she screams. "Dammit Van! That's not funny!" She jumps up and down. Her eyes water and her heart pounds so strong you can see it beat through her gray flimsy t-shirt. "Why aren't you scared?"

"Language!" Gran swats her spoon on her pot.

For the first time, Tamara's tough girl act isn't on display. She's normally the shit talking, pot smoking, first to swing in a fight one. But the presence of our dead ancestor has exposed that she has a vulnerable side. A side of her that I've never seen in my seventeen years, or thought I would ever see being that she is the eldest and has always presented herself as unfazed.

"I'm sorry, Tam. Stop crying." I reach over the table and hold her hand.

"Tell Gran to take back what she said about me being touched."

Snot runs down her nose. Gran hands her a paper towel from the handle below the kitchen window.

"If *ya* touched, *ya* touched. There's *nothin'* you can do about it. The gift is in our blood. You aren't the first, and you won't be the last."

"But I don't want this—gift—as you call it. I want to be normal." Tamara cries with sad, red eyes and a runny nose.

"Well, maybe since you're denouncing it, you won't be visited anymore. I'll pray on it tonight." Gran looks at me. "What about you?"

I crack the top of my strawberry soda and take a bite out of my peanut butter crackers. With a mouth full I reply, "I'm not scared."

Gran smiles at me from the corner of her mouth. Tamara scratches the dried tears itching her cheeks. The glass in front of her slides a millimeter to the right. She freezes at the table.

"Relax," I say. "It's just condensation." I lift the glass from the table to reveal the wet patch. "See? Why are you so scared all of a sudden?"

"Because it's not the first weird thing to happen to me."

"*Whatchu* mean?" Gran turns off the stove. She taps her pot with her spoon, then makes her way over to Tam. As she wipes her hands on her apron, the cabinet door with her seasonings makes a creaking sound and slam shut. "Oh, Lawd."

Tamara looks at me. "I'm getting outta here."

Gran places a hand on her shoulder as our eyes shift between the three of us. My sister's whole body shivers. Gran places her other hand on her and leans down to comfort her with a loving hug.

"I thought I saw something in here one time before, but I couldn't say anything," Tam confesses.

"Why not?" Gran asks.

"Because it was the day you found my weed, and I thought you were going to say I was stoned and lying. But I wasn't high. I know that now. Those things really do exist."

"What things?"

I join in and ask, "What did you see?"

"I don't want to talk about it. I just want to get out of here. I wish Mama would hurry up."

Gran squeezes Tamara's shoulders, then kisses her cheek. "You'll be fine, baby. You've renounced it, so everything will be fine."

Gran lies to her. I know because her eyes looped when she said that, and the pacifying tone in which she spoke was the tone she used when she lied to my uncle the day he showed up drunk at the family reunion. "Drink your life away. See if I care. But you *ain't bringin' dat* drink in here. My days of worrying about you are over," she said. But she did care. Still does. I knew it when the words left her mouth, and she just used the same tone with Tamara.

She steps back to the stove. "Vanya, set the table."

Ma walks in the house with her phone pinned to her ear. "I take it you haven't heard the news yet?"

Tamara runs and hugs our mother. Ma wraps her arms around her, then looks to Gran for answers. Gran throws up her hands, so Ma looks at me. I avoid her glare and sip my soda.

"We'll talk later," Gran mumbles, covering her pot. "What news?"

"Sit down, Ma." My mother holds on to Tam with one arm while reaching for Gran's hand with the other. "Daddy had a heart attack."

CHAPTER 2
DEATH DAZE

I cover my mouth with my hand and my eyes grow wider than a lemon on a juicer. "That's why the cabinet closed by itself," I say.

"Is that still happening around here when someone dies?" My mother looks at Gran, then me.

"It did a few minutes ago."

Gran sits in a daze, staring at the copper butter dish. Tamara lies her head on the table crying. My mothers looks off in the distance.

"Ah!" Tamara jumps in her seat when the phone rings in the living room.

Ma turns to Tamara. "What's with you? I've never known you to be jumpy."

I hop up. "I'll tell you after I answer the phone."

She nods as she rubs Gran's hand. "The word is getting around I'm sure. But Mama, don't you worry. I will handle everything."

Gran rises from the table. "I'd like to go lie down. You girls make sure you eat. Ya here?"

"Yes, ma'am."

Gran walks past me on the couch writing down the first of many condolence messages. Ma is on her heels. The long-winded caller quotes scripture, ignoring the many attempts I've made to end the call. I say thank you a few more times and they finally hang up.

"*Iihup*," I gasp. "Damn Tamara! Announce yourself when you're standing behind people."

"Sorry. I didn't want to sit in the kitchen by myself."

I shake off the jitters. "Now that it's just you and me, tell me what you saw. I promise I won't tell anyone."

"If you do, *I'mma* tell Gran you *ain't* as innocent as you pretend to be. I know about you and Ricky." Tamara folds her arms.

"You don't know shit," I say.

She leans to the side with a sly smile on the side of her mouth. "I know you've been kissing him at the park when you're supposed to be at that bogus after school program."

"Who told you that?"

"Don't worry about it. I won't tell your secret, if you won't tell mine." Tamara reaches forward with her pinky bent. "Swear."

I take the bait. I lock pinkies with her, and study her eyes before she shares her secret. She huffs and wipes her sweaty hands on her jeans.

"Okay. That day Gran found my stuff, I was in our room and this green man was in the hallway telling me to come here. I called Gran back in the room and she walked right past it. When she didn't say anything, I thought I was high. But deep down in my bones, I knew it was real."

My hands cradle my chest. "You slept with me that night, too."

"Now you know why."

I shove Tamara. "Why *you ain't* tell me then. That's the type of shit you're supposed to share."

Ma walks back into the living room. "What y'all in here talking 'bout?"

"Nothing." We both answer.

"Um hm. And what's going on with you?" She says, staring at Tamara. "Why are you so jumpy and crying and carrying on? My daddy just died. You're supposed to be comforting me. But I have to be here for mama. *'Cause* we know how this family is." Ma rants on and on.

"Ma!" I interrupt.

Her eyes cut me like a knife and her mouth balls up ready to curse me out for filth.

"I'm sorry. I was trying to get your attention."

Ma presses her lips tight and my shoulders stiffen.

"Tamara, show her so she can see."

"See what?"

Tamara grabs her phone from the kitchen and shows Ma the ghost in the window. "This was in here today. Van saw it first, then it showed up behind me."

"Did y'all show this to your Gran?"

"Yes, ma'am. She said it's her great-grandmother."

Ma stares at the screen and places her fist to her mouth. "I was hoping it skipped you two. I wish it had skipped me. Come here baby." Ma hugs Tamara. "You get in here, too." Her hands wave me in. "With Daddy passing, Great-Great-Gran probably appeared to welcome him in. It's nothing to be scared of, okay?"

We shake our heads up and down, but Tamara drops a tear.

"I know it's a lot to ask y'all to be brave, but I'm asking. We have a funeral to plan and people are gonna be in and out of this house all week. Can I count on you two to hold it together? Just for a little while." Ma nods at me then Tamara.

"Yes, ma'am," I say, for the both of us.

"We'll talk about everything soon."

"Should I wait to tell her about the you know?" Tamara asks.

I nod. Ma shifts her eyes between the both of us and loosens her grip around my shoulder. "Un uh. Tell me now."

Tamara lowers her head and drops more tears.

I confess. "She saw a green man in the house, but was too scared to tell anyone."

"Oh my Lawd." Ma murmurs and holds her chest. "You saw the Leprechaun Man."

CHAPTER 3
SHARON'S SIGHT

Within a few hours, Gran's house is packed with family, neighbors, and friends. They trickle in and out, bringing a range of emotions with them, but when Aunt Sharon walks in, a brief silence hits the room.

Tamara breaks the lull and says, "Hey, Aunt Sharon. Ma and them are in Granddaddy's room."

She walks past the stares, glares, and whispers from the kitchen and living room unbothered. She's used to the gossip and town talk. The things people say about her never affect her confidence. Never change how she commands attention in a room.

She opens the door to Granddad's room and closes it behind her. For a brief moment, cries, sniffles, and prayer escape the room. Once it's closed, our cousins and visitors return to their casual conversations already in progress. Most of them share memories of Granddad while cracking open beer some genius brought with them. Then, there were the liars, sitting around telling stories that sound too good to be true, or downright ridiculous.

I whisper to Tamara, "Remember the last funeral we went to?"

"Vaguely."

"I do. I remember listening to people talk and wondering why the stories they shared were mostly about themselves."

"Aw yeah. Like people who post pictures with a famous person when they die."

"Exactly. It's like saying, "look at me with this dead person.""

Tamara snickers. "Right. When all they had to do was post a picture of that person and say something nice."

Ma and Aunt Sharon come out of the room and wave for us to follow them outside. We jump at their command to get away from the characters showing up at the house, even though the heat smacks us as soon as one foot steps on the porch. The sun has called it quits, which makes the heat slightly bearable, but the mugginess of outdoors still has the power to curl up edges no matter how much gel you've used to slick them down.

Goosebumps prickle on my arm when the stink bugs buzz towards the lights on the porch. They fly like they're playing dodgeball, barely missing my head.

More of the family arrives on our way out. We speak to them and tell them to join everyone inside, then pile into Ma's car. She looks at Aunt Sharon with enlarged eyes that scream a story is behind them.

"Why did everyone get quiet when you walked in the house, Aunt Sharon?" I ask.

"Because a lot of people in the family are afraid of her," Ma says.

"Why?"

"Because she..."

"Why are you speaking as if I'm not sitting right here." Aunt Sharon cuts Ma off. "Because the dead speak to me."

"And *'cause* she is the only root doctor in the family," Ma adds.

Tamara and I sit back in our seats and stare at Aunt Sharon. Her eyes shift between us, and the hairs on my arms stand at attention. It's hot, but a chill enters the car like a warning to stop asking so many questions. I shut my mouth and revert to a little girl—I only speak when I'm spoken to.

Aunt Sharon says to Ma, "*Why ya* ask for privacy?"

Ma holds her hand out to Tamara. "Give me your phone." She selects the photo Tamara took. "Look who showed up in her selfie today."

Aunt Sharon studies the image and smirks while nodding her head. She looks up at Tamara with pride in her eyes.

"I sense fear. *Why ya 'fraid?*" she asks, in that serious tone she uses when she's disappointed.

"I just am."

"How *'bout* you?" She points at me. "You 'fraid, too?"

"No," I say.

"Good." She smiles. "And you saw her, too?"

"I saw her first."

"There's more, Sharon." Ma interrupts. "Tam saw what you saw when we were kids."

"I saw all kinds of stuff. Be more specific."

"She saw the Leprechaun Man."

The interest of this mysterious entity wipes the smirk off of Aunt Sharon's mouth. "Just Tam?"

Ma nods.

"Umph. Just like when we were kids." Auntie murmurs.

"*Whatchu* mean?" Tamara asks.

"This little green man would appear to me and only me. Your ma would be sitting right next to me and couldn't see him. But I could."

"That's how it happened with me. He was standing in the doorway and I called Gran in the room. She walked right past him and didn't see him."

"That's what he does. He only reveals himself to certain people, and I never figured out why. I've heard different accounts over the years, but I'm the only one in the family who has seen him until now."

"What does he want?" Tamara whines.

"No one knows for certain. I assumed he wanted to make me go crazy. Sitting in our room staring at me while your ma was yapping away on the phone looking right in his direction. Can you describe him for me?"

"Ugh. He was small, and weird looking. His face kind of shifted, like it would be glowing then turn blurry like bright green smoke. And his eyes *was* a cross between black and that same glowing green color when he showed his face."

"Same son of a bitch," Auntie says.

"I don't wanna talk about this anymore."

Auntie shakes her head. "Don't you be 'fraid of him."

"How do I make all of this go away?" Tamara asks.

"You don't. It's in your blood. And your blood is strong. We don't have weak women in our family tree. Great-Great-Gran showed herself to you because she determined you two were ready. So be ready." Auntie's voice echoes a vibration. She reaches over Ma and fumbles around in the glove compartment. "There you are," she mumbles below her breath and lifts a black velvet bag. She pulls out two necklaces. "The blue sapphire necklace will give you peace. That should keep that little green asshole away. This purple amethyst is to help you accept the awakening of your gift. Wear them all the time. In the shower, at school. Wherever."

Tamara drapes them around her neck. "Yes ma'am."

"If you need something, you come to me." Auntie nods.

I break my silence and ask Aunt Sharon, "How come the dead speak to you? Because *ya* touched, work roots, or are you the chosen one in our family?"

She laughs deep and low. "I think the spirits got you two mixed up."

CHAPTER 4
COUSIN CARLOS

As more family trickles in, Gran's house begins to feel like it doesn't have central air conditioning. Escaping the uncomfortable collection of body heat, Tamara and I join a few of our cousins under the big oak tree out back. Everyone was complaining about how hot it was inside the house, and laughing at how it was cooler outside.

The older folk separated themselves from the younger family members, claiming the tent near the shed a few feet away. Cracks of beer cans opening and fizz oozing from beer bottles combined with the night air made the old fogies rowdy. They recanted stories we never heard before. Humming in agreement if they remember certain situations. And when one name is called, all of us under the tree grow quiet and eavesdrop on the grownups conversation.

Reno, Gran's youngest brother, begins to tell the story of how Aunt Sharon kept Cousin Carlos out of jail with her magic. Even the crickets and beetles stop chirping and buzzing loudly when Auntie's name is called—Similar to when the lights go out in the movie theatre and everyone sits still and quiet waiting for the big screen to light up the auditorium.

Cousin Carlos sits across the yard on the back porch with one of his lady friends. They say he doesn't touch *the drink*. Every now and then I've seen him smoke a joint with our Uncle Wayne, but I never saw him drink anything in a red cup, or from a coated colored bottle.

It was too crowded and too dark to see who shouts, "Aye Carlos, come tell them what Sharon had you do when you were hustling!"Judging by the slurred speech and vibrato, it sounded like our jailbird uncle Popcorn egging him on.

Carlos points to glowing, yellow eyes. "I ain't coming over there with that black cat hanging around!"

Popcorn throws his empty beer can at the cat. It screeches and hisses at him. Its yellow eyes shine brighter like two small suns, then it glides away slowly down the hill behind the shed.

Cousin Carlos comes over with his friend and they sit at the edge of the bench. He looks down and draws squiggly lines in the dirt with his car keys with every eye in the backyard piercing into him. We all quiet down, watching his face turn pensive.

His lips twitch before he says, "I don't think y'all need me to tell y'all Sharon is the truth. All of us out here got a touch of something in us. It's heavy in the bloodline, but *dat* Sharon— Man she kept me from going to prison and jail so many times. The first time she saved my ass was when I had to bring product back from Mexico. She gave me and my running partner two protection powders."

"Why?" Reno's wife, Eileen asks.

"Shhhh." Many of us mouth as a collective.

Carlos looks at Reno to keep his wife quiet then continues. "As I was saying, Sharon gave me and my partner a brown glit-tery powder in one jar, and a greenish looking powder in another jar. Each time she gave it to us, the brown jar was always bigger than the green one. She told us to rub the brown powder on the outside of what we *was* transporting, and put the green powder in our pockets."

"Say what now?" The lady visiting with Carlos asks.

"I'm telling the truth. I wouldn't be sitting here today if I had *got*' caught in the airport *dat* day. The real fucked up part is, we had taken *dat* trip so many times, and it always ran smoothly. Nothing ever went wrong. We'd land, check into a room, grab some food at the same cantina, and wait for our contact to lead us to the meeting. After we made the exchange, we'd go back to the room and do what Sharon told us to do."

"Every time?" Eileen asks.

"Every time." Carlos confirms. "But the last time we *was* down past the border, the jars Sharon gave us *was* bigger. Like she knew we *was gonna* need more of whatever it was she concocted. Man! *Dat* last trip...Shit went sideways. We always picked the slowest hour to come in and leave, but *dat* day traffic was bad as fuck. And then when we finally *got to* the airport, it was dogs everywhere. I ain't never seen canines at the check-point. I told my partner, "Look man, we need to take a loss on this one. I say we flush it and get back to the states. I ain't doing time in Mexico. No sir.""

"Hell no, you don't wanna do no time down there!" Reno adlibs.

"But my partner trusted Sharon. He convinced me to follow the plan and I did. When I tell you those dogs went **crazy** in the airport when we approached the gate. The cop owners didn't know what was wrong with them '*cause* they couldn't pinpoint what was setting them off. They ran around in circles, barked, whimpered—Didn't stop until we made it past checkpoint. The whole time I was wheeling my bag, I was wiping my forehead with my shirt. Sweating like a turkey in November."

All of us laugh out loud while Carlos shakes his head with a grin on his face. Eventually he laughs at his own joke with us. I assume his memory of the incident replays in his head and gets to him.

Eerily, the same black cat climbs up the tree behind Carlos and sits on a limb facing the adult circle. Reno notices it, too. He cackles before guzzling down his beer, then reaches in the cooler and opens another.

"If y'all think that's something, you *ain't* heard shit yet. Tell them about the river and the talking cat." Reno sits back with his feet resting on a cylinder block.

"Now you're just telling tall tales now," says Carlos's lady friend.

"Ain't no tales coming from me. If I wasn't scared, I would put my hand on a bible right now. But I don't play with religion *no mo*. I speak the truth." Carlos raises his hand to scout's honor.

"A talking cat?" Eileen denies his story with laughter.

"Reno, they can't handle it man. *Dat* one is too much for them. Hell, it's still too much for me." Carlos's voice lightens. "I don't know what the fuck I was thinking *doin' no* shit like *dat*."

Popcorn eggs him on again. "*Tell'em* cousin."

Murmurs surround the tent. "A talking cat…He gotta be *lyin'*…I don't believe nothing he's saying."

Carlos says with his chest, "Which *youngblood* said they don't believe me?"

His question is met with silence.

"*Whatchu youngbloods* know about voodoo?"

CHAPTER 5

RIVER ROOT

All of us *"youngbloods"* as Cousin Carlos calls us sit quietly. I know of roots—Or rather have heard of it in passing from time to time. Some of the elders call it voodoo and hoodoo, but it has always been a hush-hush, taboo topic they whisper about, which of course piqued my interest.

I never ask questions when I hear roots being discussed. I sit quietly and take mental notes of what is being said. And I'm smart enough to know better than to raise my hand and answer Carlos's question, *"Whatchu youngbloods know about voodoo?"* I know very little, but just enough to convince me it's not my wheelhouse.

The yellow eyes of the cat sitting in the tree radiates brighter in the silence. It appears to have eased closer behind the elders in the tree, too.

Carlos continues, "Y'all youngins must know something about it, because you all got quiet. Over there sittin' still as a frozen lake." His mouth hangs open laughing at us.

"Leave those *churn* alone and tell them about the talking cat," says Reno.

"Alright, Reno. Calm down." Carlos motions with his hands. "I have to paint the full picture. My partner in crime, Skoob, heard about a hoodoo ritual this other root doctor could perform to make you gain power, provide protection, and bring you good luck. Hell, we needed it in our line of work. So, I asked Sharon about it and she refused. More like warned me really. So, I went to the lady Skoob told me about down in Horry County. He warned that what she gonna have me do is I had to do was pretty fucked up. And I quote, "Los man, the shit she *gon'* tell you to do is *gon'* sound crazy as hell, but I did it, and I swear I feel different.""

"Yet you still went through with it?" Carlos's lady friend frowns at him.

Carlos fans his hands at her. "Pearl, please. We've all done dumb things. And if you've never been in the streets hustling, you wouldn't understand."

Pearl's eyebrows furrow. "And what fucked up thing did you have to do? Be mindful, I drove you over here. You may have to find a ride home."

Carlos looks at her with a blank stare. As the tension rises between them, the rest of us suck our teeth at this woman's threat.

Popcorn kills the silence. "Hell, he's over here with family. Someone will make sure he gets where he has to go. Go on finish your story, *Cous'*!"

Light chuckles murmur in the darkness. Pearl folds her arms and Carlos toots his lips at her and continues.

"This lady examined me head to toe. After staring in my eyes, she told me it was many ways to fulfill my request, but these steps were required to bring me the most luck and protection. Brace yourselves. It gets wild and requires the magic bone of a cat."

The cat in the tree suddenly sits taller. Its yellow eyes narrow as it inches closer to the edge of the branch.

Carlos leans forward and stares at the grass. "Late one night, I had to catch a cat and boil it alive at midnight by the riverside."

"Say no more." Pearl jumps up from her chair, speed walks to her car, and leaves tire marks in the driveway.

Carlos shrugs his shoulders and confesses. "It wasn't my finest hour. Anyway, my instructions were to hold the cat upright in the boiling water until the bones break down."

"Now it all makes sense why you avoid cats," says Popcorn.

"Oh, he ain't nowhere near finished!" Reno adds.

"Yeah, listening to the cat shriek and holding it still in the water gives me nightmares to this day. The night sky looked down on me. The moon was shining pretty and bright, but once that cat started hollering and screaming, grey clouds came from out of nowhere. But somehow, I went through with it, and boiled that cat down to its bones. The voodooist said you would be able to tell which bone was the lucky one because it would stand out from the rest. I couldn't tell the difference. This was the first and last time, I might add, that I ever did some shit like this. So, I had to follow her next step. I threw the bones in the river and waited."

"Waited for what?" asks Tamara.

I pinch her on the arm. She flinches and narrows her eyes at me. She doesn't need to say a word for me to understand I should never pinch her arm again.

"When you throw the bones in the river, you wait for a bone to flow back to you upstream." Carlos says, looking over his shoulder.

I assume he senses something near to him. I look up in the tree, and the cat has magically disappeared. I'm not sure how I missed it move when I was fixated on its glowing eyes.

Eileen asks, "Did one flow upstream?"

Carlos nods. "Fucked me up when it did. Flowed right back to where I was standing. I picked it up out of the water and wrapped it up in a cloth like the voodooist told me to and remembered her words clear as day. "Keep dis *witchu* at all times. No harm can come to ya.""

"I believe you sold your soul to the devil, Carlos," says Eileen, drawing a cross in the air in front of her.

A collective gasp echoes from both ciphers.

Cousin Carlos replies, "Well since you're such a saint, you should be alright then. Huh?"

"Reno, are you gonna allow him to talk to me like that?"

"Go in the house." He points to the back porch. "I'll be ready to leave in a short."

His lips tighten after he takes a swig of his beer. His wife sashays away from story time and we dive right back in.

"Did you feel a difference like your friend said?" Popcorn asks.

"I felt more than a difference. Skoob and the root worker failed to mention the drawbacks of sacrificing the cat."

Suddenly the black cat from the tree appears next to Carlos and jumps in his lap. Now **he** was frozen like a lake in winter.

The cat sticks out its tongue and turns its head side to side. Carlos stares at it with stretched eyes, barely taking a breath. I watch their interaction closely. He doesn't blink while the cat glares upon him. He appears to be in a trance with the cat's movements. When it finally stops, it tilts its head to one side, stretches its mouth wide, then sits upright holding its stare on my frightened cousin.

The buzzing of the bugs disappear into radio silence. The trees stop moving as if there is no night air. The cat grins at Carlos then jumps down beside him. It strolls a few feet back towards the hillside, looks back at Carlos once more, then takes off into the woods.

"What the fuck was that?!" Popcorn exclaims in a whisper.

"So none of y'all heard what that cat said to me?" Carlos exhales, still unable to blink. He closes his eyes and repeats his question. "Did anyone hear what that cat said to me just now?"

Our circle looks at each other in confusion. The elder circle keep their eyes on Carlos, staring at him like he's losing his mind. The quiet doesn't last long as someone drives up blasting their radio.

"I didn't hear anything, Cous." Reno hands him a beer. "But it's good to see you blinking again."

Carlos pushes away the can and shakes his head. "Y'all just witnessed one of the drawbacks of me *foolin' up* with someone besides Sharon. I should have never stepped outside of the family."

Popcorn asks, "What would happen if you tell us what the cat said?"

"That's just it. I'm forbidden to repeat it."

"Why?"

"I don't know! It just warns me I can't repeat what it says." Carlos wipes the sweat dripping from his forehead. "And I'm not about to be Curious George and find out."

"And this ain't the first time a cat has talked to him either," Reno adds.

"When was the first time?"

Carlos looks at the young circle. "A few days after I boiled the cat."

Reno sips the last of his drink. "Now what he's 'bout to tell y'all is what he told me. I was skeptical at first. Thought *Cous'* was high on his own supply."

A collective laugh escapes everyone's lips, familiar with the lyrics of Biggie Smalls' song.

Carlos waits for the snickers to die down then says, "I'm not gon' lie. I was feelin' myself the mornin' after the night by the river. There's no way I can put it into words except I kind of felt like a King. Like my shit didn't stink."

His description of the after effect earns a few more chuckles. The intrigue of his story makes us forget about the dry heat while we wait for another breeze to shoot by.

"A few days later, I went to check out my people on my other side of the family up in *North Cack*. Everything was cool on my visit until my cousin's took me over to one of their friend's house. We were sittin' downstairs laughin' and jokin', when suddenly a voice whispered in my ear. "Who said that?" I asked them. The three of them raised their eyebrows and made a funny face at each other. The voice said something else so I asked them again. "Which one of y'all is saying that?" The three of them looked at me like I was crazy. The girl whose house we were visiting asked me, "What did you hear?" And when I went to open my mouth to tell them, the voice reappeared closer in my ear and said, "Don't repeat what I say to you to nobody." I was spooked because no one was standing next to me. I jumped up and looked beside her couch. *Wasn't nothin'* there. "Y'all are playing a trick on me!" I yelled. They all had stone faces, and my cousin's stared at me with concern begging me to sit down and collect myself. Next thing I know, the friend's cat eased down the stairs real slow. And this I can repeat. That cat sat on the bottom step, shined its yellow eyes, and said to me clear as day. "You heard me talking." I hopped up off that couch and told my cousins, "We gotta get the hell outta here now!" I wrestled with the door, and it wouldn't open. We were in a rough neighborhood and I didn't pay attention that my cousin's friend had to put the key in the deadbolt lock at the top of the door to get out."

The sound of fear in his voice brings laughter to the young circle. It shouldn't, but that's the lack of compassion and unseriousness of my generation.

"You *youngins* are so disrespectful," says Reno.

"*Sholl* is. Ain't shit funny *'bout* what I'm telling y'all. You better take heed and not fuck around." Carlos chastises us.

"You really expect us to believe a cat spoke words to you?" Young Dee says, sitting at the end of the bench in our circle.

"It talked to me and told me, "You asked for this. Welcome." I can't repeat the rest. Honestly, I don't know if I could because I never tried. I've obeyed what it said to me and kept its words off my tongue." He looks at the time on his phone. "If it wasn't so late I would call my kin and let them tell you how that cat started acting crazy for no reason when I was *tryna* get *outta* there. The girl said her cat ain't never acted like that before. It had to be what was on me."

Popcorn mutters, "The cat bone?"

Carlos nods. "The damn cat bone was in my back pocket. I kept it on me at all times like the root lady said."

"And how long did the cat talk to you?" Reno asks.

"Until the girl put the key in the lock and let me out of her house."

I chime in. "I believe you."

Everyone turns to look at me.

"Thanks, lil' cous'. Which one are you again?"

"Vanya," I say. "We all saw how that cat was acting strange in his lap a second ago. Why don't y'all believe him?"

Young Dee adds his two cents. "It's a tad outlandish. *Don't cha* think?"

I sigh. "Have you ever had a cat act mysterious, hang out in a tree and listen to people talk like they could understand the conversation, magically disappear, then reappear out of nowhere and jump in your lap?"

"Hell naw."

"Well that's what just happened. I saw it with my own two eyes."

Cousin Carlos pats his chest. "And now y'all have seen first-hand why I don't fuck with cats. I'm scared of *them* things."

Eileen rejoins us. "Y'all still out here listening to Carlos tell lies?"

Some of us mumble at her presence. The rest of suck our teeth loud enough for her to hear she isn't welcome.

She huffs. "You ready yet?"

Reno stands to stretch. "I guess. It is getting late. I'll holler at y'all tomorrow."

His exit triggers the rest of the family to follow his lead and call it a night. As we *youngins* and the elders disperse, a few of us fold the chairs and pick up the empty beer cans the elders missed when targeting the black plastic garbage bag tied to the end of the table. Popcorn and Young Dee joke around, admitting they believe Carlos's stories, but didn't want to seem gullible.

"Don't they say cats are the keepers of the underworld?" Tamara asks.

"It depends on the culture. One culture believes a cat symbolizes female divinity and good luck, another believes they are evil creatures. I've even heard some cultures believe all souls are transferred into cats when people die." I shrug. "Who knows which one is true."

Uncle Wayne walks up and cracks the last beer in the cooler. He empties the melted water near the base of the tree.

"What *was y'all outchea* talkin' 'bout?" He asks, with an unlit cigarette hanging from his mouth.

"You wouldn't believe us if we told you, *Unc'*," says Young Dee.

He strikes his match against the wooden picnic table. "Try me."

"Carlos and his stories about roots and magic cat bones and talking cats."

"Umph." Uncle Wayne scoffs. "Did he tell you how Sharon kept him from doing life in prison?"

CHAPTER 6
GREAT GHOST

The day Granddaddy died brought a slew of family and friends over to Gran's house. Ma says we can expect many more throughout the week.

"We're gonna spend the night here with Mama. She shouldn't be alone with so many people stopping by, and someone has to be here to tell *straglers* when to call it a night," she says.

Tamara's shoulders slump after she kicks the air with her feet. She begs Ma to let her stay home alone, but Ma isn't hearing it.

I place my arm around her. "We can bunk together tonight. Okay?"

She looks at me with big eyes and sighs. "I'm not sleeping in our room."

Together we pull out the guest bed hiding under the sofa in the den. Uncle Wayne flings the back door open and scares the shit out of us.

"Whooo!" Tam belts and jumps.

A cloud of smoke trails behind him.

She spazzes with her hand across her chest. "I thought that door was always locked?"

"It is. I went out for a smoke. I'll lock it back. Why are y'all pulling out the sofa?"

"We're sleeping over to be here for Gran," I say.

"What's wrong with your room?"

Tamara and I look at each other.

"It's for guests." I lie.

Uncle Wayne raises his brows. "I'm not giving up my room." He shoots past us telling us Aunt Sharon and Ma not to volunteer his bedroom to anybody.

They fan him off and continue their conversation. Uncle Wayne interrupts them again.

"Hey Sharon, did you hear Carlos was outside telling them about your hoodoo?"

"Telling who?" Aunt Sharon asks.

"He had a whole audience out there."

She scoffs. "And?"

"How 'bout a cat was out there fuckin' with him." He chuckles.

Aunt Sharon, Uncle Wayne, and Ma burst into laughter at the same time.

"Serves him right." Aunt Sharon moans. "Going to someone outside of the family."

"You ever gonna get him right?" Wayne asks.

"I might." She laughs.

Uncle Wayne points to Ma. "I was telling your two to ask him how Sharon kept him out of prison."

Ma counters. "Why don't you tell them how she saved your ass from that crazy girl in the north area?"

"Pipe down, Regina. Those two think the world of their uncle. They don't need to know my street business."

Ma and Aunt Sharon laugh at him in his face. Uncle Wayne folds his arms and gives them the big brother stare down.

Ma chortles. "Everybody knows your street business."

Aunt Sharon begins to say, "Who doesn't know you're the biggest man wh...," but she's interrupted.

"Now whoa whoa whoa," Uncle Wayne says, with a curve forming on the side of his lip. "That's character assassination."

Not even **he** can keep a straight face with his rebuttal. Everything being said was the honest to God truth, and they laugh with each other until Ma brings up another memory.

"Whatever happened to that crazy girl?"

"I wouldn't know. After Sharon and Mama took care of her for me, I never heard from her, or saw her again."

"That was the point." Ma fans her hand. "Good riddance."

Uncle Wayne changes the subject. "When is Junie getting in town?"

"Tomorrow night." Sharon sighs. "Guess we better get a good night's rest before the sheriff and the bride of Satan arrive."

The mention of Uncle Junie's arrival shifts the energy in the room. Tamara and I pretend we aren't listening in on their grown-up talk and pat the edges of the bed flat when Uncle Wayne and Aunt Sharon walk by.

"See y'all in the morning," they say.

"Good night."

We avoid Gran's room once the house settles. Her baby sister and cousin stay over in our room, while Ma sleeps in her and Aunt Sharon's old room. Tamara and I whisper in the dark, unable to fall asleep with the grandfather clock in the living room ticking loudly and donging every hour.

3 a.m., we've been quiet for a good fifteen minutes. My eyes

begin to feel heavy and I assume Tamara is also on her way out. Then, suddenly Gran's bedroom door opens. Tamara's leg moves below the covers. I pretend to be asleep, watching Gran float by us in her white nightgown. Her steps are quiet. Mute even. She looks heavenly in the moonlight shining through the big window on the opposite side of the den.

Tam and I lie frozen under the covers, waiting for her to come back through the room. Every hour the clock rings, but there's no sign of Gran. I assume she can't sleep, the same as us, and decided to make herself comfortable in her favorite chair near her sewing machine in the front room. I assume many other things regarding her whereabouts. *'Is she in granddad's room? Did I fall asleep for a few minutes and miss her walk back by?'* I wonder.

Seven o'clock in the morning, the clock strikes so strongly that the old wood cracks. Gospel music serenades the rise of the sun slowly revealing its splendor above the trees in the big window when Gran's clock radio alarm also sounds off in her bedroom.

I yawn, struggling to get out of bed to shut it off for her. But then the music stops. She steps out of her bedroom and walks toward the den. I squint my eyes and pretend to be asleep as she covers us with the blanket resting at the foot of the pullout.

I tremble at the sight of her. She's wearing her green striped nightgown and her hair is pinned with pink sponge rollers. She carries on into the kitchen and turns on the faucet, filling her coffee pot with water from the sink. Pots and pans clank, waking the entire house. Shortly after her daily pot of grits, oatmeal, scrambled eggs, and bacon veils throughout the house letting everyone know that she is up, so you have to get up.

Tamara finally turns to face me. "Did you ever fall asleep last night?"

"No. Did you?"

Her head moves side to side. "Did Gran ever go back to her room?"

"I didn't see her come back this way."

Tamara's heart rate increases rapidly. Her pajama top bounces against her pounding chest. Her eyes stretch wide staring into mine.

"Then who the hell was that lady in white that walked past us last night?"

CHAPTER 7
WAYNE'S WOMAN

Tamara swirls her spoon in circles in her grits until they form cold, hard mounds. Neither of us have the gumption to ask Gran if she changed her pajamas, did she leave her room last night, and if so, when did she walk back through?

We sit quietly at the breakfast table with Gran and her sister, Aunt Lois, talking about the arrangements.

"*Who got* the body?" Great Aunt Lois asks.

Ma walks into the kitchen. "Swinton's. Why are these two so quiet?"

Gran shrugs her shoulders. "They haven't said a word all morning."

Ma frowns her face while our second ghostly encounter ate away at us. The silence in the room makes it impossible not to hear Great Aunt Lois slurping the hot coffee from her mug. We shift our eyes towards her, simultaneously annoyed. The phone rings and drowns her out like a merciful instrument.

"I'll get it!" I say.

Volunteering to answer the phone calls is just the distraction I need to not think about the woman in white. Not that I'm scared. *I for one* hate when it's quiet, and the deathly silence in the house makes me uneasy—Seeing Gran in her mourning state doesn't help either.

Tamara leaves the table to fold up the bed and shower while I play secretary. I shortly follow behind her and get dressed, then search for her to see if she's ready to talk about it.

"Have you seen ,Tam?" I ask Uncle Wayne, sitting on the bottom step of the front porch.

He points to the side of the house. "She's out back smoking the roach I left on the window sill last night."

"*Okaaay*," I mumble.

"Gonna be a scorcher today," he adds, then opens the newspaper.

I walk around back and Tamara jumps at the sight of me.

"Oh. It's just you."

"Yeah. It's just me. You *wanna* talk about last night?"

"Nope. I want to forget any of these weird things ever happened. And I'm not sleeping over here tonight. I love Gran, but this is too much for me. Weird cats, ancestors, and leprechauns lurking in the shadows playing games with people's minds. I'm over it." She exhales the last bit of Uncle Wayne's joint and steps on the bud.

"You can't run away from what's in you," I say.

"Watch me. I'm denouncing all of this shit."

I sigh a deep breath of exhaustion from the lack of sleep. "Uncle Wayne knows you're back here smoking his shit."

"He's cool. He's not like the rest. He won't lecture me. Plus, I need something to take the edge off."

"Come back inside. People are dropping off all kinds of food and dessert. Ma wants us to manage the kitchen."

The house fills once again. Chatter in every corner, people eating and leaving plates throughout the house for us to pick up after. By the time school is out, the house has become too packed and too hot.

Tamara lies to Eileen. "Ma asked if you would watch people and serve the food while Vanya and I run to the store?"

"Run to the store? What for? The store is practically in this kitchen." Eileen points to the spread overflowing on the table and countertop.

"I'm just telling you what she said."

"Hurry back." She fusses.

We slip outside and walk up the block to the weed man's house. Tam slips him a ten dollar bill for a dime bag and hides it in the sole of her sneakers.

"Here. Give this to your uncle." The weed man passes her another dime bag. "And I'll know if you gave it to him or not."

Tam grins at him and nods, then places the other packet in her other shoe. "Let's roll," she says, marching off with more pep in her step.

The sun cooks us during our walk back. We skip going back in the house and join the crowd from last night already gathered out back. I grab blocks of ice from the cooler filled to the brim with beer. I drop one cube down my shirt, and rub the other cube across my forehead. Tam swipes a red cup from the table and fills it with ice. She smirks when I draw up at her crunching on every piece with her mouth open.

My face scrunches up until Uncle Wayne walks up. He stares at Tam taking her time to swallow.

"Oh. Somebody told me to give you something."

He holds out his hand. "Then give it to me."

"Not until you tell me what Aunt Sharon was talking about last night."

Cousin Carlos is closely standing by and chimes in. "What *was* you and Sharon talkin' 'bout last night?"

"About how she kept you out of prison."

"Yeah...That's not the story I wanna hear." Tamara crunches on another piece of ice. "I wanna hear about you and the crazy girl *y'all* were talking about."

"Oh, I remember that," says Carlos. "Yeah, tell them 'bout the situation you got yourself into."

Uncle Wayne places one hand on his hip and shakes his head at Tam. "To be bribed by my favorite niece."

"Hey! I'm standing right here," I say.

"I mean one of my favorite nieces. Guess I taught you well. *Whatchu* wanna know?"

"Who is the woman and what happened?" Tam demands.

Uncle Wayne lights a cigarette, cracks open a beer, then sits in one of the beach chairs. "Now take what I say as a lesson of what not to do in your little—ugh—personal relationships. I'm talking to all of you. As you may know, I like my substances, that's no secret. But I also like a lot of women."

"That's definitely not a secret," Reno mutters. "You took my woman once."

"Water under the bridge, Cousin. Water under the bridge. As I was saying, I met this gal out in the club. She *wasn't no* real looker, but hey, she was something to you know...y'all get the picture. So I went home with her the night we met in the club. She gave me the goods and breakfast in bed in the morning. I didn't have my stash on me so I slept on over past breakfast. She didn't complain and fixed me a hot lunch. That was my first mistake."

Young Dee pulls up a chair. "Why?"

"Because I didn't see her cook it. And every man should know not to ever eat anything red from a woman if you didn't see her cook it. Remember that when you become a man. My second mistake, not leaving her house with everything I came with. After I spent that first night with her, I kept going back. That was unlike me. I mean your uncle pulled some baddies back in his day, and this one wasn't one *of'em*, but there I was with my nose wide open at her house every night."

"If you knew Wayne back in those days you knew that was out of his character," Reno tells us.

"That's right. I was a one and done kind of fella, but not with *ole* girl. Then I made my second mistake." Uncle Wayne shakes his head. "I let her do my laundry."

Everyone present shares a look of confusion.

Young Dee speaks for all of us. "Why was that a mistake?"

"*Ya* see boy, first she got me in her hooks with that spaghetti she cooked. Second, she got me to where I didn't wanna leave her with my laundry. Now one thing about your uncle, I ain't never been into drama. I ain't fought with no woman, begged no woman, harassed no woman, or ran behind no woman. But I would fight this woman all the time. *Ya* see, that's what she liked. We would fight, argue, cuss each other out, I would leave and come home for a few hours, then go right back over to her house. Something wasn't right."

"When you say fight, do you mean you put your hands on a woman, Uncle Wayne?" I ask.

"As much as I hate to say yes, yes. I didn't fight her like another man in the street or nothing, but I would have to fight her to get her off of me," he says, then lifts his shirt. "You see this scar? This scar is from when she cut me. I made my way out of the house and called your mother to come pick me up. The doctors sewed me up and I told Regina to drop me off…Guess where."

"Surely not back to that woman's house."

Uncle Wayne laughs. "*Ding, ding, ding.* We have a winner. Regina and I got into a huge argument. She put me out on the side of the road and I walked my ass right back over to that crazy woman's house. The next time I came to visit Mama, she looked me over real good and called Sharon over. Sharon took one look at me and told me to spend the night at home. I refused. Cursed Sharon out for filth. She looked at Mama and nodded her head. Next thing I knew, Junie and Daddy came at me and held me down until I fell asleep."

"What did that do?" Tamara asks.

"Nothing. It's what Sharon did. The family said my feet wouldn't stop running in my sleep."

"Running how?" I ask.

"Literally running. Running in place."

Reno clears his throat. "Wayne was passed out asleep and his feet were moving in the running motion." He winds his balled fists. "It was like he couldn't rest because he had to get somewhere."

"To that lady's house?" Tam says, in the form of a question.

"Yup. Sharon and Mama took off my shoes and put cayenne pepper in them. Eventually my feet stopped running and I woke up in the morning hating that woman. Sharon took me outside and had the dog to smell me. We went over to that gal's house and let him loose in her yard. He sniffed his way to the back and started digging. Sharon tapped me on the shoulder and said, "Watch what he pulls up." That dog dug through that dirt like his treats were buried under there. He leaned his head forward into the hole and when he came up, my underwear was in his mouth. Sharon blew the dog whistle and he came running. We came back here and threw my *drawers* in the trash can. Sharon poured salt on top, struck a match and dropped it in the bin. After that, I ain't never spent the night at another woman's house."

"And that's how the motel on the corner stayed in business!" Reno cackles.

Suddenly, Ma's voice carries across the yard. She stands on the porch with her hand on her hip and yells at us.

"Tamara and Vanya! Come here!"

"Shit," Tamara mumbles.

Uncle Wayne taps Tam's shoulder. "Now what you got for me?"

"I'll bring it back to you," she says, takes a few steps, then stops abruptly. "Uncle Wayne, what happened to the woman?"

"Hell if I know. Our paths haven't crossed since. The way the root is supposed to work, is since Sharon burned what she planted, she's supposed to have hard times fall upon her. But I'm no expert. Ask Sharon."

Tamara scoffs. "*I'ne* asking Aunt Sharon nothing else."

We take our time approaching the porch. Ma's eyebrows are furrowed from a distance, and her hand never slips from her hip as her feet tap on the concrete of the top step.

"Which one of *y'all* lied and told Eileen I said to serve food?" Neither of us answer. She rolls her eyes at the both of us. "I see. Well, go to the house and make sure it's clean. Spic and span. Especially the back room. One of you has to give up your room for a few days and bunk together. I'll let y'all work that out. Your Uncle Junie and his family are gonna pile in with us. And be back before the street light comes on."

"Yes, ma'am," we say.

CHAPTER 8

REGINA REVEALS

The sky is indigo and the street lights are on by the time Tamara and I make it back to Gran's house. Ma is too occupied showing hospitality to notice. The crowd out back is loud as they've had their fill of alcohol, and the good time they were having summons us to join them.

As soon as we step on the grass, Sharon appears behind us on the front steps.

"You two were supposed to be back before the street lights came on," she says.

Tamara whispers, "I never noticed how spooky Aunt Sharon is until now."

Auntie grins on the side of her lips as if she heard what Tamara said. "Your mother and I have been waiting on you to come back." The alarm beeps on her car and she throws the keys to me. "Start it up and turn on the air. Your mother and I will be out in a minute."

We stand against the doors while the car cools off. Ma and Aunt Sharon come outside a few minutes later and order us to get in. The two of them continue with their conversation and I listen close for clues to pick up on what they're talking about. They don't include me or Tamara in whatever secret they're holding, and the two of us sit quietly all the way to the Swinton's Funeral Home.

Tamara's eyes meet mine. "Why did we have to come here with you?" she asks.

Aunt Sharon looks back at us and unlocks the doors. "Let's go, you two."

Auntie walks inside the parlor first. Ma holds the door open for us and walks in behind me. We stand in the lifeless front room with way too much burgundy for four walls where a woman creeps up on us and leads us to the office.

Tamara and I are forced to listen to them talk to the director and his wife about home going packages, floral arrangements, and casket colors.

"Would you like to visit your father before you go?" The director asks.

We follow them to the back to view the body. Aunt Sharon and Ma hold on to Grandad's hand with their eyes closed and say a prayer. Tamara and I stand in the doorway, watching and listening to them grieve. Chills and goosebumps prickle my skin, then the room suddenly turns cold.

I fold my arms together while Ma and Aunt Sharon silently move their lips. I assume they are saying their personal goodbyes to Granddad. If not, I know better than to interrupt.

Ma's voice heightens and the vibrato in her voice makes the hair on the back of my neck rise. Sharon looks back in our direction. She focuses on me and smiles.

Ma asks, "Do either of you want a moment alone with your grandfather before we leave?"

"No," I answer for the both of us, not realizing Tamara has left my side.

I felt her presence next to me this entire time. I haven't a clue when she stepped away. And I begin to wonder, *'If it wasn't her presence I felt, what or who was there?'*

Aunt Sharon shakes the director's hands and leads us out of the mortuary. We find Tamara leaning against the pillar on the porch.

She bombards our mother and aunt. "Why did I have to come here with y'all?"

They ignore her until we're back in the car. "We wanted to see Daddy one more time before they embalm him."

"And I wanted the both of you to come to see if I was right about my hunch," says Sharon, pursing her lips. "And I was."

"What hunch?" I ask.

"I think **you** know. You felt something in there. I'm sure of it." She narrows her eyes on me.

"What? All I felt was the room get cold."

Her brows raise. "Do you know why?"

"From that look on your face I don't think I wanna know why."

Her eyes roam between Ma and Tamara. "Did either of you get cold in there?"

"No," my mother answers.

"I only got cold when the AC finally kicked on before I left," Tamara says.

"That *wasn't no* AC child. A spirit entered the room and stood at your sister's side."

"What?!" my mother shouts.

"No need to be alarmed. It was friendly."

"A spirit? Was it Daddy?"

"Un uh. I didn't feel Daddy in there for some reason. But I got my answer. For some reason the spirits got you two mixed up. But I reckon they know that now."

"And what am I supposed to do with this information?" I ask.

"What you're doing now...Being brave. As for this one over here..." Aunt Sharon points to Tamara. "Those crystals I gave her should give her a peace of mind. Especially since she called herself denouncing her gift."

Tamara shouts her question. "How do you know that?!"

Ma cuts her off with her hand raised. "Your aunt just knows shit. She just knows."

I interrupt. "Ma, why did Sharon get these "gifts"—And how do I have them, but you don't?"

Aunt Sharon dry chuckles. "Your mother has other special abilities."

"Like what?"

The Swintons blow the horn as they pull out of the driveway. Ma's eyes glisten in the lights reflecting from their car.

"I have a sort of insight to things. I see images in my dreams, or have premonitions that most times come true. I just don't speak on it."

"Until now." Sharon bullies Ma with a stern look. "Tell them your secret."

"I wouldn't call it a secret. I've never claimed, or delved deeper into what it is. If *it* has a name at all," Ma says, holding her chest.

Her eyes stare off into the darkness and I follow them, hoping she will share the thoughts flashing in her mind. Patiently, we wait for the big reveal. The part of her she's concealed all these years.

Aunt Sharon huffs. "It's called many things. Clairvoyant. Psychic. Seer. Medium. Oracle."

Ma refutes. "I'm not saying I'm any of those things."

"Why?" I ask.

"Because sometimes I'm wrong. And there is nothing like being known as a fraud, or a liar, or the girl who cried wolf."

"Tell them about the times you were right." Aunt Sharon insists.

Ma releases a deep sigh and looks away through the front window. My eyes travel with hers, then I speak before Ma explains her experiences.

"Didn't The Swintons leave a moment ago?"

Tamara answers first. "Yeah. Why?"

I whisper, "Aunt Sharon, start the car."

She scowls. "What?"

"Please. Just do it. And get us out of this lot."

She doesn't question me a second time. The engine cranks and we spin out of the lot. In that moment, we bond on a deeper level. I don't have to repeat myself for her to understand, and she doesn't need to question me further as my senior.

She jerks the car, leaving skid marks on the asphalt. Once we're down the street in the grocers lot, the silence ends in the car.

"*Whatchu* see, baby?" Aunt Sharon asks, surveying every angle of the lot.

"A silhouette was staring at us from the upstairs window."

"Could have been a cleaning service?" Ma suggests.

"We were the last car in the lot, Ma."

"I know…Just trying to find a logical explanation."

"You see girls. This is what your mother has always done. A gifted skeptic is what she is. Listen to this. I remember the first time she realized she had powers. We were in elementary school and had an assembly program to witness a shuttle launch into space. It was a huge deal. All of our classmates were excited. Except your mother. She blurted out. "Something bad is gonna happen to them." I shushed her, but a couple of the other kids heard what she said. Sure 'nough, the rocket exploded on live television. I turned to my baby sis and couldn't take my eyes off of her." Aunt Sharon squeezed Ma's shoulder. "Tears streamed down yo' mama's face, and her legs and hands trembled for at least an hour. And all I could do was wrap my arms around her, because I was too afraid back then to ask her how she knew. And from that moment, I didn't see her as my little sister. I saw her as my sister with the gift."

A moment lulls between us so I ask, "Ma, how did you know that was gonna happen?"

"I didn't know for sure. I just had an image of the rocket trapped in black smoke flash in my head while the news reporters were talking. And when it happened, I felt this sharp pain in my chest. I'll never forget that feeling."

Tamara bows her head. "That's horrible."

"It was. And after it happened, I never told anyone about my flashes."

"Not even Auntie?" I ask.

"Not even me." Aunt Sharon scoffs. "Until she found herself scared shitless down in Orlando. Tell'em."

Aunt Sharon clears her throat and nudges Ma on her arm. She in turn shoves Auntie back on her shoulder, then looks at me and Tamara with lecturing eyes.

"Listen to me carefully. What I'm about to tell you, I regret my part. It goes against everything I have been trying to teach you two. In a way, what happened is the reason I am so hard on you. Okay? Don't judge me for being stupid is all I ask."

"We won't," I say, then side-eye Tam to co-sign with my response.

"We won't," she mumbles.

Ma exhales a deep breath. "Keep in mind the bible verse, '*Be careful about what you think. Your thoughts run your life.*' Now, you two have heard stories about when I tried to be a rich and famous singer before. Right?"

"Yeah."

"Well, during that time, I was out in the world on my own. Mama and Daddy didn't support my serving the devil, so they didn't give me any money whenever I called begging for their help. They called my genre of music secular. In church lingo it means songs of Satan. So, without any assistance from my parents, I had to pick up odd jobs here and there through a temp agency. I lived paycheck to paycheck, barely making ends meet, and had to shack up with whoever would take me in. Mostly between friends." She sighs. "Anywho, we partied all the time, and I spent my money on slutty clothes to wear to the clubs—Or my boyfriend's money if I had one. Just blowing money. Trust me. It was no way to live."

Aunt Sharon's face crumples. "I didn't realize you were living that bad off?"

"Y'all are hearing the glorified version. It was much worse. I spent days at a time crying, praying, wanting to quit music, but also wanting to succeed in it. It was a very confusing and sad time for me, but grace and mercy got me through it."

Aunt Sharon sucks her teeth. "Let Mama tell it, her prayers of you not succeeding were answered."

"Right. Funny how some prayers work, *innit*?" Ma rhetorically questions.

She and Auntie share a look that Tamara and I don't understand. We look on for clarification, but receive a confusing promise to explain what that meant later on instead.

Sharon sighs. "Sometimes you don't want people to pray for you."

"That's right. Some people pray against you. But that's a story for another time," Ma adds. "Now where was I?" Her lips slightly part. "Frankie. Right. Things started to shift once I met Frankie. Back then, your auntie would give me 20 to 40 bucks to hold me over. I lived on store brand turkey meat, a loaf of bread, bag of chips, and a pack of Oreos. I was destitute. And I knew it. But I couldn't bring myself to come back home and live —here."

"You lived off of 40 dollars?" Tamara asks.

"Yup. Sometimes guys would take me out to eat and I'd spend their money. But for the most part, turkey, chips, and cookies every day and every night. Then, I met your father and never wanted for anything. He supported me more than any other person in my life. He gave me one of his cars to drive so I wouldn't be stranded, filled the cabinets and fridge wherever I was living at the moment with groceries, and made sure I had pocket money when I hit the road. I'm telling you all of this because your father's contribution to my livelihood is an intricate part of what I am ashamed to tell you."

Ma shakes her wrists and blows from her mouth like she's in labor. Her chest pounds so hard you can see her heartbeat thump in the center of her neck.

Aunt Sharon wraps her hands around Ma's. She soon calms down and her shaky hands become still.

"So." Ma huffs. "During one of my road trips, your father filled my car with gas, gave me money to eat, but skimped on spending cash. I didn't need anything, but had become accustomed to him spoiling me. And I admit I wasn't happy with him giving me the *just exact* amount I needed for my trip. But I didn't complain. I wanted to, but I didn't."

"Our mother. A gold digger?"

"I was not. I said I was spoiled. I just told you how I ate turkey sandwiches to survive. It was only natural to get hooked on good living. It's hard to go from sugar to shit. Remember that. *Anyways*, on my way back home I did the dumbest thing. I stopped by the mall knowing I didn't have enough money to buy anything. I had just enough money to gas up again if need be, and buy something to eat. But there I went, depressing myself with window shopping. And of course, when you don't have any money, you see everything you want. Shoes, bags, earrings, dresses. You name it and I wanted it. I walked out of an expensive store and said to myself, '*I wish I had enough money to buy that dress and those shoes. What I wouldn't do to have them.*' It wasn't two minutes later, a red faced man in tight jeans began walking beside me. I sped up my pace. So did he. I slowed down. So did he. Then I stopped walking. So did he."

"The fuck?" says Tamara.

"Language—But the fuck is right. He grinned on the side of his mouth like the devil himself and said, "Some friends and I are looking for a good time and we would love to have it with you. You're a pretty one. We'll pay you whatever you want."

My mouth falls open. "What did you say?"

Ma is pissed when she looks at me. "I said no!" Her eyes roll and she and auntie shake their heads. "I tried to walk away and he blocked me. His face turned redder. And I could feel the evil coming off of him. Him? Or whatever it was. I took a few steps back and he took a few steps forward. He said, "You know you want to. Come on. Have some fun. We'll take good care of you. Pay you all the money you need for that dress and those shoes." If my heart could have jumped out of my chest it would have. How was he privy to my personal thoughts? How was it he repeated what I said moments just before he walked up on me? I didn't say I wanted that dress and those shoes out loud. I didn't touch or try them on, and I browsed at a lot of things in that store. Why would he specify the dress and the shoes? And he would have stuck out like a sore thumb if he'd been watching me in that store. His face was so red, you couldn't have missed him."

Tamara perks up. "So did you kick him in the shins and run?"

"No. Once the shock and fear unlocked my legs, I did an about face and prayed he didn't snatch me from behind."

"What did he do?"

"The same as before. He walked beside me continuously

complimenting me on my looks and telling me how much money I could make and have my own money for once. The more he talked, the more I realized I was in the presence of the devil."

"Come again?" I ask.

"You've heard Mama say the devil can preach. The devil is good looking. And the devil is always lurking."

Aunt Sharon adds to Gran's repetitive catch phrases and quotes. "And the devil hears your cry."

"Bingo. The devil was listening to my thoughts. His red face repeated them back to me all the while trying to turn me into a two dollar ho."

"But what happened when he followed you?" I ask.

"I walked until I found a mall cop and told him I was in danger and being harassed. He asked me to describe the man. I turned around to point to the red-face man and he was gone. I was frantic. The cop escorted me to my car and I burned rubber getting the hell *outta* Dodge."

Aunt Sharon chimes back in. "She called me bawling her eyes out. I had to take off work the next day to go see about her."

"I didn't sleep for days. And if I did it was because I collapsed. I worried he would reappear. I was scared my thoughts would summon him. And the encounter brought up all of the other premonitions I didn't tell anyone about. Like out of the blue I would see a celebrity's face, then as soon as I turn on the radio or the TV that same celebrity would be featured, or making a huge announcement, celebrating a birthday, or died."

"This one time we were dancing, and your mother started doing this MC Hammer routine." Aunt Sharon's face beams.

"Who?" I ask.

"He was a big deal in our day. Anyway, Frankie turned on the TV and guess what was on?"

Tamara laughs. "A commercial for hammers?"

"No. A special documentary about MC Hammer."

"Okay, give an example about someone we know."

"I'm afraid to tell you, but I will say recently, two celebrities were being talked about every time I turned on my television, and I got those flashes again. Sure enough, they both died."

"She's called breakups, too."

"I sure have. I've been right about each of those, but lately every time I write about a city, the city hits the news with a major tragedy. It's happened three times in the past six years. So you see. I have no way of taming whatever this is called—Or how to control it."

"Did you know Granddad was gonna die?"

"I did not see that coming. The latest flashes I've seen was a shoe being thrown at me, which felt very real. And for as long as I can remember since becoming an adult, I have had this recurring dream. I am living in this weird designed house with tall gold curtains, two front doors and a woman wearing a powder blue dress sits at the entrance and teaches students how to play the harp. I walk past her every time I use the middle entrance. She's always with a student, and we never meet eyes. And when I wake up, I am convinced I was actually in that house."

The car fills with silence. Each of us look in a separate direction, processing the events Ma is sharing with us. I sit holding my chest with one hand, and biting my fingernails on the other, trying to recall if I've ever experienced anything similar to her gift. Nothing came to mind.

Aunt Sharon breaks the silence between us and shouts. "Everybody put your seatbelts on!"

The engine revs and she leaves a second set of tire tracks on the road. The car throws us side to side as auntie nearly overcorrects the car on two wheels.

"What's going on?!" Ma shouts.

"Look at that grey Buick pulling out of the lot. What do you see?" She asks us, gripping the steering wheel tight in the ten and two position.

Tamara clicks her belt with tears welling in her eyes. "It's him!"

I turn around and look out of the back window. "Him who? I can't see a face!"

"Neither can I," says Ma.

"It's the green man! How can you not see his face?!"

CHAPTER 9

SHOTGUN SHARON

All I see is black smoke rippling behind the steering wheel. No face. Nothing green. And I'm terrified. The inside of my fingers begin to dent from gripping on my belt strap. And Aunt Sharon is driving so fast I have to hold on for dear life.

"Drive, Auntie!" Tamara yells. "He's gaining on us!"

I didn't think her Caprice had speed under the hood, but the way Aunt Sharon is running through red lights and whipping curves and curbs, I need to learn more about old cars.

Auntie can teach me if we survive this chase. She's fearless behind the wheel and appears to be the only one of us unafraid right now. Her eyes are laser focused on the road. Her tongue is hanging out the side of her mouth. Her hands are glued to the wheel. And her shoulders rock back and forth with every bump in the road we defeat. The front of the car squeaks as the engine revs like a sports car.

Aunt Sharon calmly asks Tamara, "Do me a favor, baby? Feel for a zipper on the side of your seat."

Tamara searches for the zipper, holding on to the back of Auntie's headrest. "I found it!"

"Now carefully zip it towards your sister."

Tamara unfastens the closure until it reaches the middle of the backseat.

"Vanya, slide it all the way to your side and reach until you feel a case. When you find it, pass it to your mother."

My fingers tremble until they brush against the handle. I pull out the case and give it to my mother. She takes the box and opens it with ease.

Aunt Sharon gives Tam another order. "Reach under your seat until you feel a pole, then pass it to your mother with the barrel facing up. Careful though, I can't remember if I left one in the chamber."

Tam and I look at each other with stretched eyes. She finds the ranch rifle, gives it to our mother, and she loads the barrel and cocks the gauge.

Ma rolls down her window. "Duck down girls."

She unfastens her seatbelt, turns around to sit on her knees hanging halfway out of the window, and aims the rifle. With one eye open and the other closed, Ma squints through the scope and places her finger on the trigger.

"I said get down!" She yells at us.

We drop low and cover our ears. My head is clamped between my legs, but I can still hear Ma praying against the wind blowing in her face. *Boom.* She squeezes. *Boom.* She squeezes again. My neck and shoulders tense as the sound of bullets fly past my window.

Ma asks Aunt Sharon, "Any traffic coming?!"

"All clear!"

"Move a little to the left!" Ma says.

I peep over at Tamara to see how she's holding up as the car drifts to the other lane. *Boom.* Ma squeezes again.

"*Got'em!*" She shouts.

Chills run down my spine from the ruckus. My blood is racing as if I was the one to put a hole in the demon.

"You killed it?!" I ask, overly excited and proud of my mother.

"No. I *shot out* its tires. You can look."

I lift my head and she nods behind us.

"See. He's slowing down."

I look back at the car reducing speed and sparks igniting from the hubcaps rolling against the tar. Smoke fumes from the tires as the car twists to the side of the road and crashes into a pole.

I tap Tamara on the back. "You can sit up now. It's over."

She lifts her head from her knees, afraid to look back. The trusty Caprice slows down as we stop at the last red light before the short stretch back to Gran's house.

Ma snaps the safety on the shotgun and sets it between her legs. "You girls alright?"

"Yes, ma'am." I answer. "Aunt Sharon, *how come* you and Tam saw him as green, and I saw him as black?"

"I've been wondering the same thing. What color was he to you, Regina?"

"I saw a black and cloudy figure. And when he saw me pointing the gun at him I swear he smiled and his face shifted in waves."

"Whenever it moves, its face waves," Tamara adds.

"Some things your Aunt Sharon just doesn't have the answer to. But I'll never stop looking. You can bet on that."

Auntie finishes the final stretch doing her normal speed limit of faster than the sign advises miles per hour. Gran's yard is packed with cars, so she parks at the edge of the driveway.

Uncle Wayne meets us as we get out of the car. "You pulled up in here like a bat out of hell."

We say nothing, knowing he is one hundred percent correct about the hell part.

"Did y'all hear shooting wherever y'all coming from?" he asks, crunching an empty beer can in his hand.

"I might have heard something," Ma replies.

"I take it Junie's home?" Aunt Sharon asks, looking at the expensive car in the driveway.

He scoffs. "Him and the She-Devil, and their demon spawns."

Ma asks, "Y'all haven't gotten into it already have you?"

"I'm on good behavior tonight, sis. You know where to find me."

He walks off and passes the house, fading into the darkness of the backyard. Ma and Aunt Sharon lead us up Gran's steps and pause at the door. Both of them give us a stern look.

"We already know. Keep our business, our business," I say.

"And don't let my gun come up missing." Aunt Sharon lectures.

Ma nudges us forward. "Now go inside and say hello to your uncle and his family."

Tamara and I put on fake smiles for the crowd inside Gran's house. We inch our way out of the back door, and into the company of Uncle Wayne, Popcorn, Reno, and Cousin Carlos. They sit in a circle smoking a joint, deep into a private conversation.

Uncle Wayne looks between the both of us. "What was going on with y'all a moment ago?"

"Nothing," Tamara answers. "You know why I walked over here."

He passes her a joint from the pocket on his shirt. "And don't let nobody see you. Especially that uppity brother of mine. He would love nothing more than to judge us for every little thing we do."

"Why do you care what he thinks?" Tam asks.

"I don't. But he's disrespectful when he judges folks, and I don't wanna have to get on him and upset Mama. Got it?" He raises his brows.

"Got it," Tamara says, then turns to Cousin Carlos. "Uncle Wayne said Aunt Sharon kept you from doing life in prison. How so?"

Carlos hums. "By doing some dark shit. That's how."

Tamara and I sit in the vacant beach chairs in their circle. Tamara pulls out a lighter from her bag.

Uncle Wayne fusses. "Didn't I say not to let anyone see you smoke that?"

Reno laughs at us. "These two don't remind you of Sharon and Regina when we were younger?"

Uncle Wayne points to Tam. "Like watching my youth play out before my eyes. Especially this one. Ain't scared of nothing."

I laugh to myself knowing Tamara is scary as hell, and has sold them her fake act of bravery. She doesn't even flinch because she knows I'll keep that secret.

"So, is it okay for me to tell them what happened back then?" Carlos asks our uncle.

"*Fasho*. They can handle it."

CHAPTER 10
FAMILY'S FAMILY

"In these streets, I wasn't known as Carlos. People called me Lo. It might have been a nickname, but it also described the way I was living at that time. I did my fair share of dirt, hint the moniker—I was low down. My past has red in it is all I will tell you girls, but when it came to doing time for my crimes, I had Granddaddy—May he rest in peace—And Sharon on my side."

Tamara points to Uncle Wayne. "I thought you said Aunt Sharon kept him out of prison. What's Granddaddy got to do with this?"

"I mentioned the one time she kept him out of prison when he could have been doing life on the inside. I never said he didn't eventually go." Uncle Wayne chuckles.

"Ole Lo was a *son-na bitch* I swear," says Popcorn.

"Wasn't he though." Reno cackles and claps his hands.

Cousin Carlos looks at the men of our family reminiscing about his past struggles. He lowers his head with a look of amusement, regret, and shame on his face, then picks himself up and stares in our direction.

"I know what you girls are thinking. Your Cousin Carlos doesn't appear to be the type of guy to have such a colorful past."

"Trust. That is not what we're thinking," I say, then tap Tamara on the arm.

We giggle for a few seconds, then stop when Tam pounds her fist into her chest twice. "What she means is, we won't judge you." She throws him the peace sign.

"Cool. Y'all are like my lil' sisters. I don't want you two thinkin' bad about your favorite cousin." Carlos clears his throat. "So the story goes like this. On occasion I was arrested, spent a night or two in jail, but none of my charges ever stuck in court. I had good lawyers—Hopefully you girls won't ever find yourself in a court of law with lawyers who are supposed to have your best interest in mind. Anyway, the reality is they're all smoking cigars in the judge's chambers together like a fraternity, and making backdoor deals about yachts, vacation homes, and golf bets while your freedom hangs in the balance."

"That was a mouth full, but noted. As you were saying," says Tamara.

"Ole Lo," he says, speaking about himself in third person, "Violated his probation and got himself in a tight situation."

"How?" I ask.

"That's one detail I'll never repeat to anyone, and hoping God forgives me when I need to cross the pearly gates. The evidence was stacked against me and the prosecutors planned to trunk my case."

"What does that mean?"

"The court was going to add in all of my offenses and present them to the judge and jury to make me look like a complete monster. They even had several eyewitness statements recorded pinning me at the scene. It was over for me—Until I went to Sharon. This particular court case required major cringeworthy actions."

"More than burning a live cat?" I ask.

He begs. "Please. Don't mention that cat."

I purse my lips shut and touch Tam on the leg. When Carlos isn't looking in our direction, I point to the black cat eavesdropping in the tree. Neither of us tell him that his enemy has returned. We let him continue to speak of the unthinkable acts Aunt Sharon made him commit.

"So one week before my trial, my lawyer warned me. "The case is not going well. Expect a guilty verdict, but I'll work on the sentencing being heavily reduced," he said. I didn't believe him. Neither did my gut. I left his office and went straight to Sharon's house, desperate and nervous with one week of freedom left. I waited on her porch so long, my shirt and trousers were dripping wet by the time she made it home. She took one look at me, shook her head, and waved for me to follow her inside. I told her everything I knew and everything the lawyers said. She told me to stay out of trouble and come back in two days when the dead would be ready to work for me."

"The fuck?" Tamara covers her mouth.

"Sharon was cutting it close wasn't she?" Reno adds.

"Hell yeah. Five days of freedom left, but I never questioned Sharon. She gave me another concoction in a jar. And what she told me to do with it was whew!" Carlos hollers and shakes his head side to side real fast. He takes a deep breath and forms a curve on the side of his mouth. "Our cousin, your aunt, and your sister Sharon, told me to take the jar to a graveyard. My instructions were to find a burial with a tombstone and punch the head of the grave three times, then the feet, then the waist, then the head again. Next I had to dig a hole and bury the jar inside that very grave."

My mouth falls wide open. "That is twisted."

"Wicked," Popcorn mutters.

"Some sick shit," Reno adds.

Carlos throws his hands up. "Call it whatever you want."

Popcorn hops up from his chair and bends over to rest his hands on his knees. "Cous', you weren't scared to dig in the grave?"

"You *gotdamn* right I was scared. But not scared enough to not do it and avoid that 4 by 4 box."

"And you believe the dead really worked for you after you went punching on *dey* grave?"

"You tell me. The day of my trial had to be rescheduled due to the paperwork not coming together. Two weeks later, my lawyer and I showed up to the courthouse at nine in the mornin' like they said. We waited and waited. My name never got called for trial. My lawyer went to check on things and somehow, someway the trial docket with my name on it was nowhere to be found. My day in court was postponed yet again, while the copies of testimonies and past cases were compiled against me as the prosecution's evidence. Well that day never arrived. Two weeks later, his office went up in flames. Burned all of the testimony and case files. I never went to trial for those crimes and got off *scott free*."

"Man you lying." Popcorn punches the air. "That's how you got off?"

"That's how I got off. That time."

Popcorn's voice squeaks in disbelief. "So when you did time, what was it for?"

"Sheeeeeet. I served time cause Granddaddy threw his hands up with me. After I beat that charge with Sharon's help, I promised him I wouldn't get in *no mo* trouble. And I had calmed down for a lil' while. But then this stupid ass tried me one night on my way to the corner store. I beat his ass for running up on me, ended up in cuffs, and his family who stood by and watched me kick his ass testified against me. Normally during my hearings, Granddaddy would be seated in the back wearing that black brim hat. He would do a hand signal to the judge and I would walk. But when he heard I was in trouble again, he came to the jail and told me, "I'm wiping my hands of you son." He held up his hands, crossed them, dropped them, and left me behind. I looked over my shoulder during the jury trial, Granddaddy was nowhere in sight. The hammer came down and I did a bid for assault and battery, violation of probation, and aggravated assault."

"Why didn't Sharon help you that time?" Tam asks.

"Because my bail was denied once they had me in custody. They finally got me," Carlos says.

A commotion catches our attention at the front door of the house. The door flies open, and guests run outside, but I'm more in shock at the voice shouting obscenities.

"Is that Gran cussing?" Tam asks.

We run to be at her side.

Some woman shouts at my grandmother. "You had no right excluding me!"

Grans yells. "I told you! You *ain't* welcome in my house after what you pulled!"

"I should have been the first person you called!" The woman's voice shrieks.

Uncle Wayne stands over my right shoulder. "That's Aunt Mabel. What the hell is she doing coming up in Mama's house? She knows she's not welcome. I didn't even see her car pull up."

Aunt Sharon and Ma escort Aunt Mabel down the stairs while Junie stands at her side. Gran throws her hands left and right.

"He's my brother!" Mabel shouts.

"And he's my husband!" Gran yells back, lifting her heels and throws her shoe, just missing Ma's head.

"Oh shit!" Tamara and I say in unison.

The accuracy of Mama's vision shocks us both.

"Gran's shoe was the shoe Ma saw flying past her in her dream," I say, fiddling my fingers to touch Tam.

She stands next to me in silence as we look at Ma's enraged eyes staring into Aunt Sharon's. They wrestle with Aunt Mabel, being gentle yet firm to get her into her car. Uncle Wayne steps in to help, then rushes back to Gran, making sure she is okay. He and Junie take her back inside, and when Mabel's car leaves the driveway, Tam follows me over to check on Ma.

"You girl's saw that I'm sure," says Aunt Sharon.

"We saw," I answer for the both us.

Ma sucks her teeth. "Sometimes it's not that accurate. Remember that. Okay?"

"What was that all about?" I ask.

"About things that don't concern you," Ma replies and pinches both of our ears. "Go wait for me in the car. It's time we say good night."

CHAPTER 11
Haunted House

I n the big window, we see Ma and all of her siblings surround Gran. They coddle and settle her down, then Ma taps Uncle Junie on his shoulder and grabs her purse. Tam and I run to the car before she sees us snooping, and sit with the doors open like we've been waiting for her to leave.

The drive home is slow as she's in thought at the wheel. Uncle Junie follows us to the new house we've lived in for two years now.

I struggle not to meddle in grown folks' business and ask Ma again, "Why isn't Aunt Mabel allowed in Gran's house?"

Ma sighs and grips the wheel tight. "I guess it's best you hear it from me since everyone will be gossiping about it until this funeral is over and done with." She fusses. "Your Granddaddy was no saint. And his sister is no angel. She may be old, and you two know you were raised to respect your elders, but that woman is a walking shit starter with zero accountability. Junie, Wayne, and Sharon are my full blooded siblings, but we also have a half brother and sister over in Fairview."

"Are they gifted, too?" Tamara asks.

"No. The blood of Gran's side of the family is what flows in us. Pop didn't have any gifts I ever knew of. He was known as a churchgoing man and didn't care to hear about our special abilities."

"A churchgoing man with a family on the other side of town?" Tamara scoffs.

"I don't know much about that other family. And don't care to. As for your Aunt Mabel, Gran wrote her off when she found out it was her that instigated the whole entanglement. The woman Pop stepped out with is her best friend, you see. She allowed them to use her house, all the while smiling in my Mama's face like she was her sister. Well when your Gran found out, she kept quiet about it. That is until that woman showed up on our doorstep looking for my daddy, and begging for more money than the courts awarded her. Mama beat that woman sideways down the steps, and she ain't never set foot on 23 Brooke Court again."

"Is that why Gran was always mean to Granddaddy?" I ask.

"Pretty much. And it's why his sister is not welcome in our house. That woman is slicker and meaner than a rattlesnake."

"Did you ever have dreams or visions of Granddaddy out doing wrong?" Tamara asks.

"No chile. I mean I did, but I don't want to claim that."

"So you did?" My voice drags as I badger her.

"Like I said, sometimes you keep things to yourself because not everyone will believe you. And when it came to that other family, I never saw their faces, but sometimes I would have dreams of Wayne, Junie, Sharon and me playing in the yard, and these other three kids would ask if they could play. I never thought anything of that dream."

Tamara coughs under her breath. "It's another one out there?"

"*Whatchu* say, girl?" Ma furrows her brows and looks at Tam in the rearview mirror.

"That means it's another one out there y'all don't know about."

"You hush your mouth!"

"I'm not saying anything wrong. I'm doing the math according to your dream."

"And I told you it's not accurate all the time. And what happens with me is not just visions. It can also be a gut feeling. Like an inner voice spoke to me clear as day a few years back that said, '*Stay home. Don't go out of town. Cancel your trip.*' I ignored it and almost died in a car accident."

"For real?" I ask. "Why haven't we ever heard that story?"

"Some things you don't want to relive. And that was one of them. That entire weekend was a waking moment for me." Ma's face scowls and tears form in her eyes.

"How so?" Tam asks.

"I've never told anybody everything that happened that weekend and I never will."

My eyebrows rise as I turn to look at Tamara's reaction to Ma's response. I gesture with my eyes for her to get the story, but she sits there with pity in her eyes for our mother.

'*What could be so horrific she won't tell anybody?*' I wonder.

The garage lifts and Uncle Junie pulls his car in the open spot next to Ma's car. He and his family step out of the car and stretch.

Ma opens the door to the house. "Come on in. The girls have your rooms set up."

Junie presses his lips together then smiles. "I'm impressed. So this is what writing will get you in this town."

"In this town?" Ma scowls. "Stop acting like you ain't from here and come in the house."

"You still doing that thing where you manifest what you want?" Uncle Junie chuckles.

"What does he mean by that?" Tam asks Ma while bringing in one of the baby's bags.

Uncle Junie replies instead, "Oh, your mother hasn't told you how she thinks of stuff she wants to happen and it happens. Like the car she's driving. Seven years ago she said to me, "I see myself driving a white Cadillac."" He looks over at Ma and spreads his arms wide.

I stare my mother up and down. "Did you? Ma?"

She hugs on Uncle Junie and grins. "Ignore him and go inside."

"Un un uh," says Uncle Junie. "Your mother had a crush on this video disc jockey when we were younger. She said and I quote, "I want my husband to look like him when I get married."" He pulls out his cell phone and leans back for a better view of the screen. Slowly he types, squinting his eyes at the result. "There he is," he says. He turns the screen for Tamara and I to see. "Tell me that man doesn't look like your father."

I stare at a man with my father's face, but not my father's eyes. Tam takes the phone and studies the image with tears glazing the corner of her eyes.

"I miss him so much," she mumbles.

"Junie! Stop making my babies sad and get in the house!"

Uncle Junie takes his phone from Tam's hands. "Sorry, girls. I didn't mean to upset you."

"You didn't. Ma is just being Ma," I say. "Can I ask you something?"

"Shoot."

"Why are y'all staying with us and not with Gran?"

"Have you met my brother Wayne? Sure you have."

"Then why not Aunt Sharon's? Our house is newer, but her house is bigger."

Uncle Junie is suddenly overcome with seriousness. "Only Sharon's gypsy ass would stay in that house after what happened in there." He clears his throat. "It seems my sister has kept you two sheltered. Good for her."

Timing is everything, and I can't help but wonder why all of these stories were hidden from us until now.

'*Did the elders think we couldn't handle the knowledge of our true selves,*' I wonder.

As Uncle Junie and his family settle in, Tamara and I spend a moment alone with Ma in the kitchen.

"You crack the eggs, and you grate the cheese," she orders.

Keeping us busy has always been her way of deflection, but putting us to work was not going to take our minds off of the photograph of the man that resembled our father—Or our uncle's remark about Aunt Sharon's house.

We crack shells and grate, waiting for the perfect time to kill the silence. Since her lips are slightly poking out on the bottom, her nostrils flare and her chest sinks every time she takes a breath, I shy away with my questions. Ma's DON'T BOTHER ME FACE gets nothing but respect from me. And Tamara...Most of the time.

Uncle Junie's wife, Zu, enters the kitchen. She loads her bag of breast milk in the refrigerator, then tells us good night. Ma scoffs when she hears their room door close, then dumps the sliced spinach in the bowl.

"Did you do that because she didn't offer to help?" Tamara asks.

"Mmm hmm," Ma hums.

"Finally, we're talking. I was going crazy listening to Vanya struggle to get that white stuff out of the eggs."

I roll my eyes at Tamara, knowing she can't prepare the eggs faster than me. "Is that why you and Aunt Sharon don't like her?"

Ma twists the nozzle on the faucet. "It's not that *I* don't like her. I don't like how she refuses to do anything whenever they come around, nor how my brother slaves after her. I mean no shade and no harm, but I can't stand laziness as you two well know."

"Yes we do." Tam slides back a few steps before she feels the heat from the back of Ma's wet hand.

"Enough of that," Ma says, in her stern voice. "And let's not talk about our guests—While they're in our home."

The bedroom door down the hall reopens and closes again. Uncle Junie's voice carries while he talks to his eldest daughter and middle son playing in Tamara's room. As the sound of his conversation with them grows closer, Ma's message is emphasized with squinted eyes.

Uncle Junie stares at the back of Ma's head. "Is she still hot with me?"

Tam and I shrug our shoulders. He makes his way over to the sink and wraps his arms around Ma.

"I didn't mean to upset you lil' sis. But you can't be too mad at me if you're making your famous quiche. You know it's my favorite."

Ma rolls her shoulders. "Get off me, boy."

They horse play with each other. First, they wrestle with each other to break up the bear hug Uncle Junie refuses to release. Second, Ma starts off a round of taps once she breaks free of his hold. She settles the score by landing a wet dish rag on his arm.

"Shit, Gina! Okay. Okay. You win. You win." Uncle Junie holds up his hands to surrender.

Ma stops her attack and says to us, "One of you wash the dishes while I mix."

Uncle Junie takes a seat at the counter next to Tam. "In all seriousness, Gina, *why'you* get mad when I bring that up? I give you my word I won't do it again, but I would like to know why it upset you."

Ma's shoulders slump. "It just freaks me out. My feelings are all over the place lately. I'm not so sure I can explain it."

I lightly scrub the pans and bowls, listening to her reasons. Uncle Junie taps his fingers, then intertwines them in front of him.

"Is it because he looks just like that man from the TV, or because you still have no closure?"

"Junie!" Ma stops mixing. "As of late, it's a lot of *things* happening around here. What I do know is, I hate hearing that story about manifesting Angelo into my life, but when it comes to finding him, *I've got* nothing. Not one clue. So stop telling that story. Okay?"

"Have you cried yet?" he asks.

"No. Have you?"

"No. But it'll come when I least expect it. It always does."

A car door slams outside. They pause their exchange.

"Who could that be this late?" Uncle Junie asks. He hops off the bar stool and peeps between the crack of the curtains beside the front stairwell. "What does Sharon want this time of night?"

Aunt Sharon knocks hard and loud enough to wake the neighborhood. She huffs when Uncle Junie opens the door.

He questions her. "What brings you by at this hour?"

She lightly pushes him out of her way and scowls.

"Nice to see you, too, Sis. As always." He mumbles and hides his bottom lip beneath his top lip.

Ma grabs snacks from the pantry while the quiche bakes, and spreads them across the counter. "I didn't know you were stopping by tonight?"

"I wasn't planning on it. But after you left I finally found what we've all been looking for." Aunt Sharon pulls out a stack of folded papers from her purse.

Ma eyes the documents. "Is that Daddy's will?"

Aunt Sharon nods. "And guess who he left as executor?"

Junie takes a seat at the end of the bar. "Who?"

"Wayne." She grins.

"Well, he was always Daddy's favorite." Junie sighs.

Ma and Aunt Sharon look at him with puzzled eyes and whimsical facial expressions. A burst of laughter escapes their mouths as Uncle Junie sits looking dumbfounded with his hands pressed against his cheeks.

"How can you fix your mouth to say such a thing? We've all played second to you when it came to Daddy," says Ma.

"And it's a good thing. Even though *you were* his favorite, he knew Wayne would be fair," Aunt Sharon adds.

"But Mama is still living so everything goes to her anyway."

Ma reaches for the papers. "True, but Wayne will divide whatever money Daddy left between the four of us and Carlos, since he and Mama raised him in the house with us. He is practically our brother."

Aunt Sharon raises a brow. "What about *them other* two though?"

Uncle Junie grunts. "He better not give them shit!"

Ma nods. "I agree."

Aunt Sharon takes a deep sigh and looks around the room. She reads the faces of her siblings, then adds in her two cents.

"I kind of agree with you two."

Uncle Junie scoffs. "What do you mean kind of?"

"Don't get that tone with me. I *ain't* scared of *ya* big man voice. I mean just what I said, in a way I feel they shouldn't get anything out of respect for Ma. On the other hand, haven't those poor bastards had it bad enough all of these years. Should we slight them even in their father's death?"

The conversation amongst the elders falls silent. Junie storms out of the kitchen and treks back to the bedroom. Ma buries her face in her hands and lies across the counter.

Aunt Sharon mumbles, "That's exactly why Daddy didn't leave him in charge."

Tamara butts in. "Aunt Sharon, *Unc* said something happened in your house a long time ago. What is he talking about?"

"After what we went through today, you still have to ask that question?" She looks at Tam exhausted. "And how did that come up anyway?"

"I asked him why he chose to stay with us since your house is bigger, and he said you were the only person who would stay in that house after what happened in there."

Aunt Sharon sucks her teeth, and fans her hand at the empty chair where Uncle Junie was sitting before he stormed off. "His scary ass won't even stay at his own mother's house."

"Why not?"

"Because of the woman who walks the house at night in white."

"You mean Great-Great-Gran? The one in the photo Tamara took?"

Ma raises her head from the counter. Aunt Sharon coughs under her breath and shares a look with Ma. The look is simple at first. Then, Aunt Sharon shakes her head as her eyes stretch at me. They are having a conversation without saying a word.

"You didn't tell them, did you, Gina?"

"Nope."

"Babies, the lady in the photograph you took is Great-Great-Gran. The lady in white is not." Auntie gives a second to process that revelation. "She's a tricky one. She looks like Gran, but I'm convinced she takes on different appearances. When Junie saw her she was a white woman. She sat on the edge of his bed and stared at him until he pissed himself. When I saw her she looked like Mama, but older, and was reaching for my hand. Which reminds me, if the dead ask you to go with them, don't go. Okay?"

I nod my head while Tam covers her face and mutters into her hands. "Lord, please let these crystals keep the things in which they speak away from me."

"He will, baby girl. God is in control." Ma comforts her.

"Pardon me for asking, but why have you two kept these things away from us?" I ask.

"I was hoping you were spared. No mother wants to see their child afraid like this one." Ma points to Tam. "Or burdened with what some call a gift and others call a curse."

"I don't think of it as a curse," I say. "And I also wanna know what happened in your house, Aunt Sharon."

"My house is haunted. Many years ago it used to be what they called a log house, and a child froze to death inside."

"How is that possible? It's always hot down here."

"Every blue moon a winter storm comes through here. And like the fog, it takes lives with it when it passes. That year, no one was prepared for what was coming. It snowed six inches and the town was without power for four days so I'm told. The parents went to check in on their daughter one morning and she was blue. Apparently, the fire from the coal exhausted and the little girl died of hyperthermia. Very sad."

Tamara's voice trembles. "So why do you live there?"

"Because of what happened, it was very affordable. I renovated the property for a little of nothing."

"So, you and Gran both live in haunted houses, and didn't think to share that with us?" I glare at my aunt and mother.

"Tam and I both saw the woman in white last night. We thought it was Gran."

"What did she do?" Ma asks.

"Floated down the hall."

"That's it?"

"Yup. We didn't know it was a ghost until Gran walked past us to make her coffee."

"Well." Aunt Sharon sighs. "Like I said. Ignore her. And on that note I'm gonna turn in before the rain starts."

Ma offers, "You could spend the night here. I'll give you a gown."

"Thanks, but no thanks. But I will stop by in the morning for some of your quiche."

We clean the kitchen and push in all of the chairs once Auntie leaves. Mama turns off the lights, except the one above the stove. We say good night to each other and head down the hall to my bedroom.

After an exhausting day, I'm ready to shower and hit the sack. I ask Tam if she minds if I clean up first.

"I'm afraid to be alone, Van. Can you sit in the bathroom with me while I shower?"

"Sure," I say, hating to see my tough sister turn into a soft pile of dough made up of fear.

An epiphany comes to me while I keep her company. The steam from the shower clouds my trance in the bathroom mirror where I see us attending different schools in the fall, opposite of what we planned. Tamara looks happy and at peace—Not afraid like she has all night.

If separating for college means the powers surrounding us will bring her peace, I want that for her. She shouldn't be burdened by our family gift. It scares her too much. I hate seeing this version of her. Tortured and afraid.

I'll do anything for you sister. Whatever it takes.

CHAPTER 12
HERMIT HANNAH

Tamara and I eventually fall asleep. Taps of rain hit the house and wake me while Tam sleeps through it. As the taps turn to heavier pats, the house vibrates and the windows rattle from roars of thunder.

I sit up and rest my head against the headboard. Flashes from my blinking clock next to the bed read six a.m. We lost power some time *over in the night*. If the time is correct, there are two more hours of darkness. My mind is restless, jumping from one thought to the next. Images of my father, the car chase, the apparition in Gran's house, and the story of the little girl dying in Aunt Sharon's house.

I hold my hands close to my chest with her in mind, sad for her suffering and the loss of her presence in her parent's life.

Two streaks of lightning light the room. I count the seconds before the thunderous booms sound.

'*That was two miles away,*' I say to myself.

I tuck back beneath the sheets and cover my head. Eventually, the storm pounds on the house and puts me back to sleep. When I wake up a second time, everyone's in the kitchen munching on the quiche Ma prepared last night. Uncle Junie flips his famous pancakes Ma has bragged about for years.

"Just in time," he says. "Sleepy head gets the first one."

They're exactly as Ma described them. Buttery, light, sweet, and crunchy on the edge. I fill my belly with three of them before we pack into the cars and head over to Gran's house.

The storm was nasty but served as a blessing, giving us a break from the heat, slowing down the traffic coming to pay their respects, and forcing the small crowd of family to sit in the house together. Especially Uncle Wayne and Uncle Junie. They disappear into Granddad's room and close the door.

"If we hear a tussle from back there, just let them go at it until they tire out. Then, maybe things will get back to the way they used to be," says Gran.

My tongue burns, dying to question what the two of them are at odds about. But Ma knows Tam and I so well, that when I'm about to overstep our bounds and pry into their past, she gives me the deadliest look. I'm reminded to be quiet, and I do exactly that.

A car pulls up in Gran's driveway. "The rain is gone, but the storm ain't over," says Ma, looking out of the window.

"*Why you say?*" Gran asks.

The people in the car knock on the door, but stay outside even though Ma invites them in.

"We can't stay," says a woman wearing a turban beneath a hoodie, cooling herself with a church fan.

She passes Ma a store bought cake, and talks with her head hanging low, never lifting her face during their exchange. Ma gives her a hug, then brings the cake to the table.

"Hannah said to tell everyone hello and she was sorry for our loss." Ma finds a place on the crowded table to set the cake. "Sharon, she wants to talk to you outside."

Aunt Sharon blows out a rueful breath and steps outside.

Carlos and Reno look at one another and mumble under their breath.

"What's that you say?" Tamara asks.

"Nothing," they answer.

My sister and I roll our eyes at them. Carlos eases his way out of the house, then Reno goes to the back room with our uncles.

Ma and Gran stand at the window whispering. Tamara stands closely behind them eavesdropping, while I slide out of the back door to go find Carlos.

I find him tilting the wet seats near the shed. Fresh rain water drips down the legs. I grab a roll of paper towels from the stacks Gran stores inside the shed, and help him dry the rain spots on the bench and chairs.

"You know why I came back here, right? What's up with the lady Aunt Sharon is talking to?"

"Did you see her?" he whispers.

"Not really. She keeps her head down."

Carlos grunts, then puts down the chair he's been holding upside down. He walks to the corner edge of the house, then waves for me to follow.

"Do you see why now?"

I nod. The woman holds her head down when she talks to everyone it seems. Aunt Sharon reaches for her hands. It is then where I see damage has been caused to her skin. Her eyes remain hidden from the shadow of the hood on her jacket, and I wonder how she is managing the heat when the sun climbs from behind the clouds. From a distance she bares pretty white teeth that I see when she lifts her head higher. And I understand why she is wearing the hood and keeps her head down. Her face is discolored and disfigured from burns.

I say to Carlos. "She has to be miserable in those hot clothes."

"She hardly comes out of her house, and when she does, she dresses like that to hide her face. Damn shame what happened to her face, too. She was one of the prettiest women around when I was running the streets."

"What happened to her?"

"Boo!" Uncle Wayne creeps up on us.

Aunt Sharon and the burned woman Hannah turn our way and catch us lurking. Uncle Wayne scurries off and shags ass into the shed. I duck behind Carlos as he waves at them, taking the blame for snooping by himself.

We ease away and join Uncle Wayne near the shed where Reno and Tamara sit in the chairs we dried.

"Ain't this 'bout a bitch. *Nan* one of y'all dried a chair off and is the first to sit," says Carlos.

"Why was y'all peeping 'round the corner?" Reno asks.

"This one was begging me to tell her about Hermit Hannah."

"Ooh, ooh she used to be pretty!" Reno howls.

"What happened to her?" I ask, a second time.

Carlos and I find a seat on the dried bench. Uncle Wayne lights a joint just as Carlos begins to tell the story.

"No disrespect to you young ladies, but the full story is Hermit Hannah used to be known as Heaux Hannah."

"Hole In The Wall Hannah," Reno adds.

"She was pretty and she knew it. So much so, she didn't care who she let slam if you catch my drift."

Uncle Wayne winks at the fellas. "Hannah didn't think the rules of karma applied to her and learned the hard way."

"What rules were that?" Tamara asks.

Reno raises his brows. "Don't fuck 'round and find out."

"Hannah definitely fucked 'round and found out." Uncle Wayne chokes on his spliff and his pun.

I look at Tam from the corner of my eyes, and chortle below my breath at Uncle Wayne nearly taking himself out while making snide comments.

Carlos continues, "Hannah *more likened* messed around with

the wrong husband and found out. Of all her midnight misters, she pushed up on Jon Billy Harris knowing good and well he had a wife and kids at home. And she didn't stop after that one time. She bragged about them in front of people she knew would run and tell Jon's wife, and that wife went ape-shit on her ass. They fought in grocery stores, in the club, at ball games. That feud went on for years. Jon's wife never let up on her ass."

"I wouldn't either," I say, thinking of how Gran must have felt when she learned of Granddaddy's indiscretion.

"Well, it finally came to an end when Jon's wife lost her marbles and threw gasoline on Hannah in the middle of the street and lit her on fire."

"Say what now?!" I croak.

"You heard me. Mrs. Jon Harris set that woman on fire. The people in the insurance office put out the flames with their fire extinguisher. And Jon's wife didn't run. She watched them tend to that woman and continued to shout at her. I mean, I had heard a scorned woman is the wrong woman to mess with, but damn—After that, you didn't hear much about people creeping for a while 'round here."

Aunt Sharon walks up on us and taps my shoulder. "You. Come with me."

CHAPTER 13
PYRO PRAYER

My heart flutters as Aunt Sharon leads me to her car. We sit silently while the car cools off, listening to the viral song everybody and their mama is tired of hearing play on the radio station.

"They play this damn song every half hour it seems," says Aunt Sharon, breaking the ice first.

I nod and remain quiet with my feet hanging out of the door. The AC is set to high and the windows are rolled down, but it's so hot it takes a good minute for the heat to finally escape the car, and is cool enough to hit the road.

The song takes too long to end so Auntie turns off the radio. She wheels the car out of the driveway. From the blind spot mirrors I spot Tam peeking from the edge of the house. The suspense of why Aunt Sharon chose me to go with her alone is killing me just as much as it's killing my sister—I assume.

Once the wind sucks the rest of the heat out of the car, Auntie rolls up the windows, mixing the cool breeze with the AC.

"Van, what do you know about burn victims?"

"Nothing. The first one I ever saw in person was the lady you were talking to today."

"That lady has a name, Hannah. And Hannah needs my help. Okay?"

"Okay. But what does that have to do with me?"

"Nothing or everything. I felt guided to bring you along, so we'll soon find out," she explains. "I asked what you knew about burn victims, because an old wives tale turned out to be true. The tale says when someone gets burned, the fire lives inside of them. The victims of such a tragedy rarely come outside when it's hot. The heat is too much for them to bear. Hannah has asked me to pray the fire out of her so she won't be a prisoner in her home anymore."

I had never seen a burn victim until less than an hour ago, and now I was on my way to watch one be healed of an internal blaze.

"Have you ever done this before, Auntie? Prayed a fire out of someone?"

"No. But I believe in myself and miracles, so I'll try to help that poor woman."

"Whatever happened to the woman that set Ms. Hannah on fire?"

"She went crazy. I suppose she had no choice. She lost her husband, custody of their children, and was locked up in a mental institution. She escaped and kept the news cycle busy for weeks, and no one has seen her since." Aunt Sharon clicks her tongue.

She pulls into her driveway and my heart flutters faster. Hannah is already there waiting. I speak to her and she greets me back with a nod from her already lowered head. Aunt Sharon tells her to come inside, and I follow them both down to the basement.

Auntie points where she wants me stationed. "Sit in that corner."

I bravely take my seat, curious and afraid interchangeably about what I am about to witness. Aunt Sharon and her magic, live in action.

It's my first time down here, and hopefully my last. My eyes are drawn to the weird figurines sprinkled around the room. Colorful splashes of dust on a table filled with vibrant powders in mason jars of all sizes. The blinking light above the chair where Hannah sits in the middle of the room. The framed prayers that look older than a century.

While I wait for Auntie to begin, I reflect on rumors I've heard. Amongst the clutter, I search for a chicken foot on a string, a cross, pictures of Jesus, and any sign of the devil. I wasn't sure which was in the room with us, but something was present.

Chills cover my body and it isn't from the air conditioner blowing upstairs. It's hot as hell down in the basement, and I could only assume Aunt Sharon needed it that way for Hannah to show her how much pain she was in.

Sweat beads drip from my face while Auntie works behind the counter with her back turned to us. I examine the contents stacked in trays near her work station. Decks of cards and containers of crystals hang below multicolored beads and gris gris amulets. Below the station are stacks of books and bottles of holy water and spiritual oils labeled in French. A locked glass case filled with dolls is in the next station.

'Oh shit. Aunt Sharon has voodoo dolls!'

Hannah whimpers. The heartbreaking sound catches my attention.

"Sharon," she cries. "The heat is unbearable. Please help me. Lawd please bless her hands and rid me of this sin burning me up alive, Lawd."

Aunt Sharon turns around mixing a lavender concoction in a wooden bowl. "You alright over there?" She asks me.

I nod too soon. A dry cough whirrs in my left ear. I jump up from my seat, startled as no one is there.

"Did you hear that?" I ask them.

Auntie scowls. "Hear what my dear?"

"That," I say, as the cough sounds in my ear again. "Did you hear it that time?"

"I did." She grins.

"I did, too," Hannah co-signs. "Sounded like a man coughing."

The trapped heat downstairs is no match for the coldness I feel surrounding my body. Even as sweat drips from my nose, my body is frozen solid with fear. I'm being encountered by the unknown. And I think my aunt knows more than she is letting on.

She walks over to me and traces the air around me with her hands "We have a visitor."

I gulp loudly. "What does it want?"

"To leave!" She yells, flickering her fingers towards it. "There. He's gone." She smiles at me.

I sit back down in my assigned seat, and witness Hannah's forehead tremble when Auntie draws lines in the creases with the lavender mix. As that settles, she lights candles all around the room. The one she lights in my corner takes a few times to catch the spark. When it does, she returns to Hannah and waves her hand around her entire body.

A foreign chant escapes her lips: a mix of French, Patois, and African. Eloquently she hums and sings, circling Hannah with a vibrato in her voice highlighting specific words with continuous, intricate hand movements.

I sense Auntie growing weak, but wait for her to show a sign the heat has been prayed out of Hannah. Ten minutes, maybe longer, Auntie repeats the chant and prayer. The words become familiar to me. Certain notes feel like they are connecting to me somehow.

Hannah shakes, cries, and screams. She lifts her hands and joins the prayer. When she grows tired, she presses them against her face, and I feel a force enter the room.

A sudden downburst forms outside. Thunderous roars match the rhythm of the chant. Lightning strikes in unison with the same notes I feel connecting to me. Rains beat against the old house. The heat swells in the room and I'm on fire like a wick at the bottom of a burnt candle.

"I'm the force," I whisper.

Unrehearsed, unfamiliar, and uncontrollably, I begin to sing the chant in place of Aunt Sharon. She's fallen to her knees, weakened and beaten. I take her place and circle Hannah, hollering for God to take away her pain.

The candles blow out in the room and my body stiffens with strength. My arms spread wide as the force within me guides my hands toward Hannah.

Her mouth opens wide and her body shakes violently. Then, out of the blue she sits still as night and shrieks like a cat losing its ninth life. The blinking light above her flickers between light and darkness. Bright orange and red fire regurgitate from her widened mouth and land onto my fingertips. It's warm, consumed with pain, hatred, and trauma. I feel its malignant fuel latch on to my hands as I extract the flames from within Hannah's tired body.

The storm outside rocks the house and shatters glass in one of the windows. I move as if I've done this before and forcefully throw the flares through the opening outside onto the lawn.

The candles in the room relight on their own. Aunt Sharon rises from the floor, drenched from head to toe.

She wraps her long arms around me, then jumps back like a

kid who stuck their finger on a hot stove. "Chile. You alright?" Her hoarse voice questions me.

"I believe I am."

"So am I," Hannah says, smiling and drying her tears with the back of her hands. She stands and reaches for Aunt Sharon's hand and mine. "I never was one much for the cold, but the breeze I'm feeling flow from that window is the first cool breeze I've felt in a long, long time. Seems I owe the both of you a thank you. Hallelujah."

CHAPTER 14

KINDLE KID

I escort Hannah upstairs while Aunt Sharon nails a board across the broken window in her basement. The storm eases away when I open the front door for Hannah. The glow of the sun and rays are masked behind light gray clouds with a shiny white silhouette ring, and outside smells like burnt grass and rain water. The petrichor scent rises up my nose. I inhale it like perfume just as a bright rainbow forms in the front yard. It looks like it's yards away from the house—Able to be touched and maybe find gold.

"Humph," Hannah scoffs. "I ain't never seen one up close like this before. Looks like you can walk up to it and kiss it," she says, stretching her arms forward.

"It does, doesn't it?" I reach for it, too.

We share a light laugh, then she places her hands in mine. "Thank you for helping me."

"No need for that. Glad I could."

She takes off her hoodie and closes her eyes. She smiles at the wind blowing on her face and the drops of rain falling on her from the awning. The rainbow appears even closer—Like it floated across the street when we weren't looking.

"You should walk through it," I say.

She leaves the porch and walks near it. Waving her hands through it on the way to her car. I wave goodbye and stand on the porch alone for a short while, mesmerized at the vibrant color scheme speaking to me with its presence.

Knocks from the basement break my gaze as Aunt Sharon hammers away on the wood. The smoke from the fire merges with the black hole centered in the grass near the broken window.

"There." She huffs. "That ought to hold up 'til morning."

The rainbow disappears, so I go back downstairs. "Are you gonna put wood on the outside?"

"Un uh. This will give Wayne and Junie something to bond over." She puts her hands on her hips. "You alright, chile?"

"I don't know. Am I?"

Aunt Sharon smiles at me. "I'd say so. It appears our family's powers are getting stronger with each generation. I've heard many a tale, but none have included having our very own Fire Princess. What should we call you? Kindle Kid? Heatwave? Little Light?" She shakes her head and giggles at the nicknames crossing her mind.

"But what do we do about it? Will that happen again? How did it happen in the first place? And how did you know to bring me here to do that?" I ask, too concerned to laugh at the monikers she's testing.

"You're a young woman, Van. You should have met your inner voice by now. But then again. I believe you and I hear many voices. You need to learn which one is there to guide you. To warn you. To protect you. I know the difference in the ones that speak to me, and the one that told me to bring you alone was the one I listen to every time. She's never wrong."

"I think I know the voice you speak of. I heard it when I snuck to the park one night Ma was working late, and met up with Ricky Leonard. We kissed for a long time and my inner voice told me to stop before I went too far. Sure enough he's going around telling everybody about it."

I hide my eyes from her and twist nervously side to side. I'm not ashamed of my confession. But I'm afraid to make eye contact with Auntie after sharing my wrongdoing.

"Well, I'm glad you stopped before giving Sir Brag A Lot something worse to spread besides a little kiss. But yes. That's your voice. Don't ever doubt her. You hear me?"

"Yes, ma'am." I bravely look her in the eyes. "Do we tell Ma what happened here today?"

"Baby, it ain't too many secrets your mother and I don't share. Since the storm has let up and I've gotten this window squared away, let's head back to Mama's now to tell her."

I spot two tiny orange lights in the back near the shed when we pull up to Gran's house. Aunt Sharon chuckles when she sees them. I say nothing and shake my head because I know that laugh means she sees Tam and Uncle Wayne, too.

The house has cleared significantly from the time Aunt Sharon and I left—Thanks to the storm. The visitors that remain are on their way out when we enter. My ears stand alert at laughter in the distance.

Gran is on the telephone, and Ma, Carlos, and Uncle Junie work together picking up abandoned plates and cups in the living room.

"You two took a long time to come back." Ma glares at us. "And you both look like hell."

Auntie scoffs. "Junie, I have a project at the house for you and Wayne tomorrow. Come early."

"What's Wayne *gonna* d0...Watch me work? I'll be there sometime after 7," he snarks.

Aunt Sharon looks at me and sighs. "I tried."

Tamara and Uncle Wayne come into the house smelling like Lysol and mint.

"What's going on in here?" Uncle Wayne asks.

Uncle Junie murmurs. "We don't have to ask you what was going on out back."

"Stop before it starts." Ma points her finger at her brothers.

"Gina, how are you comfortable with him doing that with your daughter no less?"

"My daughter is smart enough to do her foolishness at home and not in the street, so you worry about what's going on in your expanding circle, and I'll worry about mine."

Carlos shouts over their argument. "*Breakin'* News everybody!"

He turns up the volume on the television so loud it can be heard outside. We all quiet down and listen to the broadcast of a young woman reported missing from the next town over.

"She looks familiar. Like Fran's daughter from Evergreen," says Carlos. "Any of y'all recognize her?"

Ma trembles and drops the trash bag in her hand.

Gran hangs up the telephone. "Turn that down, Son." She moans. "What's happened to that young girl is beyond sad, and I pray to God they find her. But I have bad news."

CHAPTER 15

RESTLESS REAPER

"That was your cousin on the phone. Your Aunt Mabel died earlier this evening." Gran announces, then turns back around to face the television.

Everyone in the kitchen stares at the back of her head in silence. She sits still with her arms folded, fixated on the silenced news broadcast.

"You can turn the T.V. back up now," she tells Carlos.

Uncle Wayne blurts out. "They say death comes in threes. Somebody better tell the Lord of Loss to keep on strolling past this house."

All of the adults stare off to themselves at that statement.

Aunt Sharon sighs. "I'll arrange for a plant to be delivered in the morning." Her forehead wrinkles when she looks at Ma. "I know that face. You okay?"

Uncle Junie hums. "I remember that look. You had one of those visions didn't you?"

Ma shivers with chills while everyone else is melting and fanning their dewy faces. Tamara stares at me with red eyes. She nods for me to go to the front door, but I pretend not to see her attempt to gain my attention, and focus on the drama with our mama.

"What did you see?" Aunt Sharon asks.

Ma stammers. "A man in a red and white boat. A body. Floating in the Ashley River next to some logs. And helicopters."

"Could you make out the face on the body?"

Ma shakes her head. "Girls, let's go home. Junie, we'll see y'all at the house.

Aunt Sharon places her hand on Ma's shoulder. "I'll walk out with you. There's something you should know."

Tam steps on my heels as we're walking out of the door. "Van."

"I saw you. I'm trying to listen in on Ma and Aunt Sharon's conversation. Hold up for a second."

She nods.

I roll down the windows in Ma's car. "I promise I'll tell you everything later."

As Aunt Sharon tells Ma what happened at her house, she glances between the two of us. I feel Tam looking at me as she listens to the details Auntie shares. I sit with my head facing straight in the back seat as her and Ma look in my direction.

"You should have asked me if she could go with you, Sharon. I had to find out from Tam where she went."

"You are one hundred percent correct. I should have. But don't be mad at me. I trusted my gut and some good came out of it."

"What's good about what you just told me? This information has to stay hidden. Can you imagine the attention that'll be put on her if this gets out? And how do you know Hannah won't say anything?"

"I took care of it. Hannah agreed to keep this between us, and knows what to say if she's ever questioned. It will all fall on me," Auntie explains.

"As it should. Now. Since we know she's evolved way past you and I, what do we do?"

"Absolutely nothing. Vanya showed strength and command tonight. I don't think we have cause to worry." Aunt Sharon looks my way and winks her eye.

Tamara turns around and stares at me uncomfortably. I'm no mind reader, but I feel what she's thinking in my soul.

"You actually pulled fire from that burnt woman?"

"I'm still in shock about it."

"You know Ma is gon' kill you if she finds out you working roots like Aunt Sharon."

"I'm not working *no* roots. Everything you heard her say is was happened. And I told her about the night I went to hang out with Ricky."

Tam snickers. "Is she gon' rat you out?"

"No. Are you still gonna hold it over my head?"

"I don't think that would be wise. Especially since you can control fire and shit." She chuckles to herself.

My voice trembles. "It wasn't funny, Tam."

"My bad. I'm a little pissed I wasn't asked to come along. Guess that was for the best."

Ma and Auntie wrap up their conversation and she walks toward the car. We wave goodbye to Aunt Sharon and Ma drops down in the driver's seat.

She turns around and looks into my eyes. "You feel okay?"

"Yes, ma'am."

"I know y'all were listening. Wanna talk about it?"

"Not really," I say.

She scoffs. "Okay. But we will talk about this." She smiles on the corner of her mouth when she turns around and cranks the car.

At home, Tamara feels distant. We go to bed without having a conversation, which is unusual. We sleep with our backs to each other, listening to Ma blast gospel music in her room. The tunes of Reverend Milton Brunson normally means she's crying.

The lead singer from his choir has a voice that sends chills throughout your body. Her vibrato in Ma's favorite song, *"I Tried Him & I Know Him"*, affects me just as much as it does her. I know this is the song she listens to when she can't control her emotions about my missing father. What she doesn't know is that the song brings tears to my eyes as well. And one falls on my pillow while Tam quietly sniffles on the other side of the bed.

Hours later, I wake up screaming covered in my own sweat. My side of the bed is soaked, and Ma and Uncle Junie are standing over me with water bottles and cold towels pressed to my forehead and chest.

The room is silent but I see their mouths moving. I can't hear anything. Not even my own screams. My mouth feels dry. My hair feels wet. My chest hurts like stones have been thrown at it all night. Then, everything goes black.

CHAPTER 16
FIRE FEVER

Nothing. No one. But something is present around me. The sound of water slowly drips from a leaky faucet in the distance. It leads me to twist and turn in the air.

'I'm floating.'

I faintly watch the arms of my pink nightgown sway about at my sides. I'm surrounded by black matter and coldness below my air born body.

"What is this place?!" I shout into the darkness, only to be met with silence.

My trembling body spins around in the wide open vastness of absolutely nothing. My voice echoes and I hear my faint heartbeat thump against the backdrop of pure stillness. My chest hurts from fear. I close my eyes as a way to cope with the obscurity. When I open them and am still in the dark, tears fall from my eyes. The ones that don't land on my cheek never make a sound below me. I convince myself this is a nightmare. That I will wake up and there will be light. That I can see. That I am safe.

"This has to be a dream," I mutter, over and over. "This has to be a dream. This has to be a dream."

"It is not a dream," a light voice whispers in the night.

"Whoever you are, I can feel your presence," I say, turning about like a lost child to find the direction from which the woman's voice came.

It grows stronger and closer. "Then, you're progressing."

My bare feet suddenly land on a cold surface. I hop where I stand. Bounce unsteadily as my heart races from fear. Not knowing what I'm standing on, or if it will disappear like some trap door and I'll free fall into the abyss, or a pit of everything I am afraid of. The worst scenarios cross my mind.

'God please don't let a snake cross my feet. Please don't let me fall off a cliff.' I pray to myself.

Slowly, I balance myself on my tippy toes. I take baby steps as disturbing images flash in my mind of horrific clown faces, mutilated ghosts, the green man, and the image of Ragnar Lothbrook's death scene in a pit of snakes.

'My God. Which is worse? The pit or being trapped in darkness for eternity?' One of my tears falls on my feet and I gasp. *'I don't wanna find out.'*

The song Gran sings as a soloist in church escapes my lips. I hum the melody at first, then whisper the lyrics to *'Order My Steps'*. My heartbeat slows a little more, and my heels finally touch the cold surface.

I'm as still as a broken clock until a sliver of bravery finds me. I take one step forward, using my toes to feel for a clear path— Still praying I land on a safe space.

"I was waiting for you to lose that fear. You don't show it often," the voice says in my right ear.

I turn and reach toward the sound. Nothing is in my grasp. That frightens me because of how close the voice was, but still I hold my composure.

"Aren't I allowed to be afraid?! Walking in darkness?! Why am I here?!"

"Because you're finally awake."

My Great-Great-Grandmother appears before me under the halo of a dim light. Her silhouette matches the apparition from the window. Her face is a mixture of Gran and Aunt Sharon. Nutmeg and angular. Shoulder length hair with a tight curl on the ends.

I hold my chest. "I recognize you. Your Gran's grandmother. Why are you haunting us? Damn." I throw my arms. "I forgot Aunt Sharon told us not to talk to the dead."

"She's right. But that rule applies in the other world. Not this one."

"Am I dead?" I grip the back of my neck with both hands.

"No. You're traveling. Follow me."

She leads the way towards a minimalist shade of red light. With each step the darkness fades. I elevate from the cold black floor to a crimson loft.

"Hurry. We have a short window of time to visit," my G-3 says.

"Who is we?" I ask. In my peripheral vision, I notice yellow eyes gaining on us. "You mean that?" I point behind me.

Great-Great-Gran yanks me by the sleeves of my gown and pulls me into the light with her. *Click.* I hear an entrance shut, but can't see a door.

"What was that? And how long has it been lurking?"

"My sweet *chile*, something is always lurking. I believe you've always known that. We are never truly alone."

The space of demure red light compels me to think out loud. "Dear God, I'm in hell."

"What do you know of such a place?" G3 purses her lips.

"I know it's a place I don't wanna go."

"Vanya, you're not in hell. When we're in that other world we are taught to believe in the things we are told, and ignore the truth which flows inside of us. You've been conditioned to believe red and black represents bad. Especially black. Let go of that nonsense. Light comes from darkness. Darkness is black. Black is beautiful and the base of everything. Make sure you teach that to your sister."

"I will."

"Now that you're experiencing your awakening, you need to remain fearless. Calm your mind and embrace your power." Great-Great-Gran stared into my eyes. "You can control fire, *can you not?*"

I nod.

"That is why red has always been your color. You represent the divine."

"What am I supposed to do with this fire ability?"

"You are more than a spark to a flame, and you were chosen because you have a good heart. Our family has had its share of *supernatural powers,* but most have been kept secret. Until now. Sharon has exposed you. That doesn't surprise me though. We thought she was the one with our family's greatest gift, but she hasn't always chosen to use her talents for good." G3 sucks her teeth. "We believe you're different."

"Aunt Sharon's been nothing but good to me, and who is this we you speak of?" My brows furrow.

Great-Great-Gran's eyes twirl, then she huffs. "Your ancestors are all around you. Now come."

I search the room for these ancestors as the room's red light turns to a bright shade of salmon. G3 opens her hands wide, and the room at the funeral parlor holding my grandfather appears.

I recognize the smell of alcohol and chemicals blended with air freshener spray, and lilies as I pace the floor. My feet aren't cold anymore. The beige carpet is rough and warm. The temperature in the room is the same. The burgundy walls and decor still stand out like a sore thumb, but being in a place close to home tapers off my anxiety.

"The last time you were here, Sharon wasn't honest with you. She saw an aura. She couldn't see a face. The cold draft you felt on your neck was indeed your grandfather. He needs your help."

My eyes grow bigger than a nickel. "Why? How can I help him? What am I supposed to do?"

"He needs you to free him."

CHAPTER 17

GOLDEN GLOW

I'm revisited by the cold. My grandfather stands across the room looking at himself in the casket. The snazzy look he used to have about him is gone. His vibrant smile's been replaced with a solemn straight line. He is completely gray. His brown skin is muted ash. And he looks like a stone man that shocks me when he moves toward me.

"It hurt me to my core you couldn't hear me calling your name the other night," he says. "All of my girls came to see me."

"I felt you, but didn't understand. I'm sorry. I guess I wasn't ready for whatever this is." My voice wavers. "But I see you now and hear you're holding on. I assume this is what they call purgatory."

Granddaddy's words hesitate leaving his mouth. "Whatever and wherever it is, I don't wanna be here. I'm not ready to move on. I wasn't ready to die."

"No one wants to die. We're all sad you aren't with us anymore." I sniff and squeeze my nose, aggravated with the smell of chemicals growing louder by the minute.

'How can I smell that?' I wonder.

G3 appears behind him and gives me a nod. Tears well in my eyes and knots form in my chest. I don't know what's expected of me. If any of this is real, a dream I'm stuck in, if I've teleported to a celestial plain, or how this ordeal will end.

I hold my head up and straighten my shoulders. "Granddaddy, do you know why I was called here?"

"No. But I'm glad you are. I always liked our talks. Not that I didn't enjoy talking to your sister, but I knew you were actually listening." He chuckles and gains a little color.

I smile at his compliment and nod at what he said about Tamara. "Don't take it personal. Tam doesn't listen to anything or anyone."

"The one thing I wanted for you girls was to not make the same mistakes I did. Or accept them from anyone." He drops his head. "I'm not perfect by far."

"Is this about the family you have on the other side of town?"

He scoffs. "Of course they're already talking about it. They've always talked about it. I just stopped listening."

I lift a brow. "I love you, but I'm on Gran's side."

"As you should be. She didn't deserve what I did to her. I tried to make it up to her, but some mistakes are permanent. As is her resentment. Now I'm stuck here and won't ever know if she forgave me."

"Would you?"

Granddaddy shrugs his shoulders and drops a tear. He declines to dignify my question with a reply, and walks back over to the casket. "And look how they have me dressed. Is this what I deserve?"

"That look is temporary. Ma will get you right."

G3 touches my shoulder. "When they are like this, it's mostly denial. But he's holding on to something. It's interfering with his transition."

I say to my grandfather, "What else is on your mind?"

"I told you. I'm not ready to go."

"I'm picking up on that. But there is no going back. You're a church going man. I know you know this. Do you want to stay here in the gray, instead of crossing over?"

"I need you to tell your sister I love her. Tell her I stopped being mad about the watch a long time ago. Okay?"

"Okay."

"She stopped spending time with me after that fiasco and I'm sorry about how I made her feel. If anyone knows about making a mistake it's me. Tell her the watch is hers. I left it at my bank in a box with her name on it."

"She'll be happy to hear this. I only wish she could hear it from you."

He scrunches his face. "I wish that were so. Tell your Gran, no matter how much of a fool I was, I never stopped loving her. She was the love of my life."

The more he confesses what is weighing on his soul, his full color returns for a brief moment. He glows vibrant like he's returning to life, then continues to release his final words.

"Tell Carlos he made life interesting." His presence begins to fade before my very eyes. "Tell my boys to stop fighting and to look after their mother, and tell my girls they were always my pride and joy."

His body floats into the air, then completely morphs into his physical body resting in the chestnut casket. I walk over and look at him closely. The vivid color of his skin has mutated back to gray. The straight line is back on his face. But this time his aura shrouds his head like a broken line.

I stare at him, expecting him to open his eyes and speak to me again. But he's gone from this world now, and I'm still lost on what I am to do besides be a messenger if and when I leave this place.

My G3 stands at my side and observes him. "He's ready now. To free him, you must touch him and seal the brokenness."

"The lines shrouding him?"

She nods.

"Where do I touch first?"

"His head, then his hands, then his feet."

I take a big swallow and follow her instructions. I lightly touch my grandfather's forehead, then hold on to two of his fingers when I touch his hands.

"Thanks for everything," I whisper, then let go of his hands and touch the black slippers laced on his feet.

His grey body brightens into a pale amber complexion, and a gold ring of light encircles the casket. I take a few steps back and bawl for the first time since learning of his death. A loud shriek hurts my throat as it pulls from the depths of my chest. I weep as the gold light slowly bonds around him in the casket. And when I take a deep breath, the transition is complete.

Gran presses her lips together with a twinkle in her eyes. "You are the next great one in our bloodline."

"Who was the last great one?"

"As problematic as Sharon is, she is of her generation."

"What about you?"

"I can summon the rain. When necessary."

Slowly, her reveal switches on the light bulb in my head. "That storm at Aunt Sharon's house—That was you, wasn't it?"

She nods.

"And the rainbow?"

"That was God."

CHAPTER 18
WOKE & WINDED

Ma is at my side when I wake. Out of breath, delirious, and jaded, I gasp as I sit up in bed. A slight pain stings my throat as I try to swallow. My mouth is dry, but what hurts worse is a force in my chest from the fast pace my heart is beating.

I slowly regain my hearing. The room feels cold like in the morgue and I shiver. I've either brought that coldness with me, or the sweat that has drenched my side of the bed is giving me the chills.

"Ma," I try to say, but I dry heave, cough, and choke.

The intensity of my labored breathing continues for too long to my mother's patience. She drapes her arms around me and prays.

"Thank You, Jesus," she says over and over until the coughs subside.

Sitting high in her arms, I see the outline of my lower body drawn in the sheets. It's not gold like Grandaddy's, but seeing the silhouette makes me think of him—Of where I just left him. I release a quiet cry as the salt of my tears tinge my upper lip. My mother continues to console me, rocking me back and forth and holding me tighter than a swaddled baby.

I push away from her embrace in need of air. She reels me back in close and I submit. Her hug is healing me and slowing down my heart rate.

My blurred vision comes into focus and I see everyone standing around the bed. I make out Tam standing in the doorway and hear her sniffles like she's lying right next to me. I smile at Uncle Junie standing behind her and hear his baby hollering in the room down the hall.

Her screams sound like music to my ears, confirming I am back amongst the living. I'm no longer on the other side. I'm home…Where I don't ever want to leave again.

"Wa—ta," I mumble.

Uncle Junie passes me the bottle of water in his hands. "You alright pumpkin sprout?"

I nod and gulp the bottle half empty in a straight shot. "Cold," I add.

Ma reaches for the blanket balled up on the bean bag near the closet. Tamara passes it to her, then sits at the foot of the bed while does her best to warm me up. I lie still in her warmth, piecing together what I've experienced. Where I traveled? How I got there, and why was it so taxing?

Tamara jumps up when the wet sheets seep through her pajamas. I try to smile, but I can't. I'm too winded and out of sorts. My mind is clouded with ways to explain what I had to do and how to relay the messages I was told to bring back. I rest my head on my mother's shoulders wondering if I should tell any of them anything at all.

'*Will they believe me? Or tell me it was just a dream.*

My eyes close in search of warmth beneath the blanket. I'm too wet to find comfort, so I challenge my mother's hold of me a second time.

"Wet. Still cold."

"Junie, thanks for helping us. Give us a minute, please."

He squeezes my shoulder before he exits the room. Then, my limp body hangs lifeless as Ma and Tamara assist one another with changing my pajamas and the bed linens.

Ma smooths out the extra comforter from the closet and lies me back down. Tam lays on the other side and holds my hands with her eyes closed. Ma occupies the other side and hums herself to sleep. Tam falls off next. I listen to them rest until the sun rays split between the blinds.

I'm fully dressed when Ma awakes. She reaches for me and opens her eyes when she doesn't feel me lying next to her. Her movement wakes up Tam who then sits up in the bed.

"You ready to talk about it?" Ma asks.

"Not yet."

"You scared the living hell out of me last night. I'm glad you're doing better this morning." She hops up to hug me. "I'm here for you when you're ready."

"We don't need to talk about it, Ma. Just know we go places when we sleep."

Ma loosens her grip, leans back, and frowns. "Go where?"

"I don't know what it's called, but it's not here."

CHAPTER 19

SHARON'S SECRET

Three days left until the funeral. Gran's house feels more like a party with each passing day.

'Why do people laugh and drink and carry on at a sad time like this?'

The thought plagues my mind as people bring over more cups, more ice, and more store bought cake that everyone passes over for the home baked ones. Especially the funeral lemon cake people can't seem to stop eating.

I stay off to myself because of what happened last night. I don't want to be treated like a freak show or circus act once the word gets out. I punish myself and avoid going out back with Cousin Carlos and the usual crowd. I'm tucked away on the back of Granddaddy's truck with one of his western novels I found in his room.

"I found her!" Aunt Sharon shouts, leaning over the cabin staring at me. "Why you hiding, *Chile*? I thought *you* and me were better than that?" She raises her brow at me.

It was hard to look at Aunt Sharon after our elder told me she didn't always use her magic for good. That little piece of infor-mation makes me question the voodoo dolls I saw down in her basement, and the frightening figurines stacked on her shelves.

"You can't look me in the eyes today?" Her voice is full of agitation. "You hear me talking to you."

"I'm not hiding. And I can look you in the eyes." I glare at her briefly, then return to my book. "I just wanna be alone."

"No, you didn't just…Your mother told me something happened last night and you don't wanna talk about it. After all we've been through together these past few days."

"Some things don't need to be discussed. And some things are best left unsaid and unknown."

Aunt Sharon pinches my shoulder. "Who are you biting with that tongue?"

I shake my shoulder loose from her fingers and stare into her eyes. She reads my message loud and clear, then places her hands back on the side rail.

"Did the devil get to you, or get *into* you last night?"

"Neither, but the truth did."

She lowers the tailgate and climbs in next to me. I turn the page in my book and pray she leaves me be. Ignoring her fails. She sits patiently with her legs pressed to her chest, staring off into the trees until the tapping of her shoe wears me down.

I huff. "I have a right to want to be alone."

"I know you do. But I'm not listening to what you want right now. Especially when my niece who I think of as one of my own is mad at me for no reason. I'm not leaving you out here until you tell me what I've done to upset you."

"Fine. I don't exactly know what you did. But I was told you haven't always used our magic for good, and that bothers me. I saw those dolls down in your basement."

Aunt Sharon's eyes grow wide as outside. Her flawless brown

skin turns maroon in the cheeks, and she inhales so deep she nearly faints.

"Who have you been talking to?"

"You mean who has been talking to me," I say.

Ma walks up to the side of the truck and rests her arms on the rails. Aunt Sharon looks at her and points.

"Tell your mother what you just said to me."

I shake my head no.

"What did she say, and why are you up in arms?" Ma asks her.

"Whatever happened last night has changed this *chile*!"

"So, she won't tell you either?"

Aunt Sharon shakes her head side to side. "And is talking to me with a wicked tongue I tell ya! A wicked tongue!"

"You apologize to your aunt right now!" Ma flicks her fingers on my shoulders.

"Ow! I wasn't being disrespectful." I rub the tingling sting where Ma struck me.

"Enough of this, Vanya. Your aunt and I can't help you if you keep us in the dark!"

"All I said was someone told me she doesn't use her magic for good all of the time."

"Who is the someone?" Ma demands.

"Your Great Grandmother."

"Didn't I tell you not to talk to the dead?" Aunt Sharon taps my other shoulder.

I take a deep breath and release. "I didn't. She talked to me. And so did Granddaddy. He said he left that watch Tam stole at the bank in her name, he is proud of you both, for my uncles to stop fighting and take care of Gran, and to tell Carlos he made life interesting. Great Gran said they had high hopes for you Aunt Sharon, but you don't always use our family gift for good, and she brought the storm over your house when we helped Hannah." I exhale long and deep.

As I huff and puff to catch my breath, my mother and aunt stare at each other with blank faces.

'*They know I'm telling the truth.*'

Ma asks Aunt Sharon, "Is it true?"

She wipes her face dry. "I can explain."

CHAPTER 20
HER HOODOO

I close my book and face Aunt Sharon, fully invested in the explanation she is about to deliver. She presses her bottom teeth into her top lip and breathes out with intensity, fidgeting her nails against her bent knees.

Slowly, her shaky hands rise to her head. She pulls off her wig and stocking cap, revealing what appears to be alopecia on her scalp. Spots of hair in patches surrounding a clean, shiny, hairless head. She's pretty enough to wear a bald head and still be attractive in my opinion, but I keep my mouth shut. Because if she felt the same, she would have done so already.

"I ask not to be judged by what I look like. Nor for what I am about to say." She looks between me and Ma, then points at me. "Especially from you."

I nod, then shift my eyes to her nails digging into her skin while the heels of her feet bounce her legs and shake the truck.

"The reason Hannah sought me out, and I was eager to help her is because I was once her. Or like her I should say. Long time ago, I too, fell for a married man. Willingly. His charm was so captivating I couldn't resist him even though I knew he was married." Aunt Sharon throws her wig to the floor of the bed of the truck and sucks her teeth.

Ma looks on with fury in her eyes. My heart sinks looking at the anguish Aunt Sharon obviously has been suffering with alone.

"At the time, I knew I had the touch. I got cocky and used a spell or two to make that woman's husband mine. Silly and stupid. I know." She sighs. "Well, it would work for a short while. He would spend two to three weeks with me, claiming he had left his wife for good. Then, shy of a month like clockwork, he would leave me and go back to her."

"Mama would have a fit if she knew about this!" says Ma.

"I know. I couldn't bear her knowing what I had done. Or you for that matter. The way you're looking at me right now is why I never told you. And I tell you everything."

"I thought there were no secrets between us." Ma turns away with her arms folded.

"There are two secrets I've kept from you, dear sister. This is one of them."

"What spell did you use to make that man stay with you?"

"Sadly, I did exactly what Uncle Wayne's girlfriend did to him. I buried his underwear in my backyard."

"Well, did a dog dig it up each time he left?" I ask.

"No. Just the final time. His wife went to a root doctor and got him to leave me temporarily, but he kept coming back until I caught her with a shovel in my yard one night."

Ma glares at Auntie. "What did you do?"

"Nothing. I let her have him and his *draws*. For some reason, I didn't wanna be with him anymore. The veil was lifted and I was free of his charm."

I reach over and hold her shaking hands. "Thank Goodness."

"There will never be good from what I did. I paid for it then and am still paying for it now. The ancestors are upset with me and I'll never get my hair back."

My mother scowls at the last remark. I look on in confusion, waiting for Ma to ask the obvious question before I do. Aunt Sharon sits with her head down and arms resting on her knees. Her fidgety heels continue to bounce the truck and make it squeak under the wheelhouse.

"So how did you…"

Ma interrupts. "Vanya. Don't."

"That has to be a record for you, Vanya. Normally, you would have asked me that question quicker. You **have** changed since last night." Aunt Sharon grins. "The relationship with that man wasn't exactly over when his wife came to my house. *Ya* see, after a while he and his wife called it quits. What once brought a smile to my face, brought tears in the long run. He figured we could pick up where we left off and came knocking on my door. I entertained him for a night or two, then wanted him gone. But he refused to leave me."

"If this story leads to domestic violence, Aunt Sharon, please stop right now. I don't want that image in my head."

"He didn't harm me the way you think. There are other ways to ruin a person's life—So he learned from his wife. When I eventually got him out of my house…And my life, or so I thought, I had the sudden urge to visit him at the house he and his wife lived in. Never in a million years would I have stepped foot into that house."

"I know that's right." Ma co-signs.

"But there I was, spending every night over there like a lunatic. That wife could have come back at any time. She probably still had a key. Anyway, my gift spoke to me and said something isn't right. I let a dog sniff me and let him search the yard. Nothing. I searched his house from top to bottom for any sign of foul play. Nothing."

"Then what was it?" I ask.

"Oh it was something I hadn't learned just yet. I tossed and turned in his bed one night so bad, it felt like nails were scratching my back. In the morning I had these marks on me."

Aunt Sharon maneuvers her back from the panel and turns it toward us. She lifts her blouse and runs her fingers against the faded blemishes across her lower back.

"I waited for that old bastard to get in the shower and searched under his bed. Nothing. Then my inner voice told me to lift the mattress. The horror on my face when I did could match the ones you have on yours right now."

"What did he have under there?" Ma exclaims in a whisper.

"Nice and neatly, he had one of my nightgowns and a pair of my undies stretched out where I laid every night."

Ma gasps and clutches her neck. My mouth drops open and my book falls from my lap.

"I assume you took them and left while he was in the shower?"

"Um-uh," Aunt Sharon hums. "I didn't touch it right away. I laid back down and waited until he left for work, then I poured salt on top of both pieces, lifted them with a fork, and placed them in a plastic bag. I drove down to the riverside and dipped my night clothes in with a stick, then burned the clothes completely between rocks and stones."

"Did that work?"

"It worked for me, not for him. He became a nuisance. Harassing me at all hours of the night. Then he looked under the bed and saw I had removed his root. That infuriated him. A few days went by and I didn't hear from him. I thought I was in the clear and we were officially over. I was wrong. That fool caught me coming out of my house one day and threw dog hair into mine, and told me if I didn't come back to him I would lose all of my hair. And I did."

Mama places her hand over her heart. "Sharon."

"Aunt Sharon. I'm so sorry you went through that." Tears fall from the corner of my eyes.

"It's okay. I've made my peace with it. I started it. I shouldn't have *done what I done*."

"I wish the ancestors could swipe this away and not hold it against you," I say.

"I'm sure whatever they are holding against me is probably not what I've told you."

"Then what else is there?" Ma asks.

"Like I said, I started it **and** I finished it." Aunt Sharon smiles to herself.

"What does that mean?"

"That's the secret I'll take to my grave."

CHAPTER 21
EVIL EYES

It's one thing to melt like an M&M in the sun, and another to sit directly below it when it skates above Gran's house past noon. Tam and I sigh at how long it takes for Ma, Uncle Wayne, and Aunt Sharon to wrap up their conversation near the steps. The heat is beyond disrespectful and they feel it just like we do, but Ma has been extra clingy to me after my walk on the dark side.

Tamara whines. "Ma, my skin is falling off."

"You sure you're okay?" She asks me.

"Yes. I'm fine."

"Go 'head in the house. And don't slip off."

The irony in her statement makes me snicker because that is exactly what the three of them are doing—Tipping off to deliver bereavement flowers to Mabel's house as a gesture to keep the peace between our clan and her children after the fight.

As they pile into Ma's truck, I overhear Uncle Wayne say, "You know Daddy came back and got her right?"

"I thought it, but didn't wanna say it out loud." Ma chuckles.

"Yep. She might still be here if she didn't come over showing out the other night. She played a big part in Daddy hurting Mama. Coming to get her was his way of apologizing to Mama from the grave if you ask me." Aunt Sharon snaps.

With everything that's been happening lately, I believe there is truth in what they are saying. A dead person can come back for someone if the hate between them keeps them bonded.

'I wonder if that correlates to forgiveness somehow?' I think to myself.

Ma merges into traffic. As I open the door to go inside, a silver Cadillac turns in Gran's driveway. A sun ray turns up the heat and burns my forearm. I escape its scalding wrath and hurry inside. Gran's occupied and Tamara is off somewhere to herself, so I make myself comfortable in Granddaddy's room.

I stretch across his bed and continue to read his old western novel. Chirps from outside the window catch my attention as I turn the page to chapter three where the action is finally picking up pace. A Red Cardinal nods its head and taps the glass with its beak. I point to the book, and the bird nods its head again.

"Are you reading it with me?" I joke.

The cardinal spreads its wings wide and nods once more.

"This must be one of your favorites, *huh* Granddaddy," I say, then press my fingers on the glass.

Tamara walks in. "Who are you in here talking to?"

I gasp and jump, then turn toward her standing in the doorway with her hands on her hips. "You need bells on your shoes."

"Whatever. Who were you talking to?"

I hesitate to tell the truth. "Ummm," I say, turning back to an empty window.

'Damn, she scared him away.'

"I was reading aloud. Tam, do you remember when Granddaddy would sneak us cookies and candy through this window?"

She smiles. "Do you remember how blown away he was

when I crushed up the cookies, and mixed them in his vanilla ice cream?"

"He said ice cream would never be the same after that." I sigh. "I already miss eating late night snacks with him while he gave me life lessons to live by."

"What life lessons?"

We both grow quiet for a few seconds. I check for the bird once more, then accept it's gone.

"Is what happened to you last night something you can't tell me about, or is it so bad that I'm better off not knowing?"

I shrug. "I don't wanna go too much into detail about it. But you should know Granddaddy forgave you about that watch fiasco. You can stop carrying that weight around with you. Okay?"

Tam looks at me in confusion, then changes the subject. "I almost forgot the real reason I came in here. Did you see that guy in the living room with Gran and the pastor?"

"Not really. Why?"

"He has to be the cutest boy I've ever laid eyes on. Come see for yourself."

Against my will, Tamara pulls me up from the bed and leads me into the middle of an adult conversation being had in the living room. Gran looks at the two of us, and without making a move, she ridicules our presence.

"Pastor Moore, you know my two granddaughter's Vanya and Tamara, don't you?"

"Sure, I know them. These are Regina's girls." He points to Tam. "I especially know this one because she refuses to join our youth choir."

I roar internally as Tamara clears her throat. She gazes at the cutest boy she's ever seen sitting at his side. Gran peeps the lust growing in her eyes and scowls, but Tam doesn't see her reaction. I make a mental note to share that with her once we're dismissed.

"Maybe my younger brother, Saul, here can convince her to change her mind. He moved here to study under me as the youth pastor of our ministry. When he's ready, he can replace me behind the pulpit. I'm sure the church would vote for him."

"Good luck with that." I scoff. "Nice meeting you. Gran, I'll be reading in Granddaddy's room if you need me."

I do an about face and excuse myself. Tamara stays behind and toys with the pastor about reconsidering the option to join the choir.

'Why is she lying to the preacher of all people?' I say to myself as I walk away.

The action in chapter three of Granddaddy's novel calls for my undivided attention. I lift the footrest and sit in his lounge chair against the wall. The soft leather swallows me and I sink in.

From this side of his room, I can clearly hear the conversation going on outside between Carlos and the usual bunch. I laugh at one of Carlos's puns, and lose my mark on the page. Then, I hear Tamara using her sweet voice, introducing Saul to our family out back.

I peek from the base of the window, smirking at Tamara twisting and turning her body about while she flirts with the new boy in town. My eyes are glued to the two of them like a hawk floating in the sky searching for prey, and the look of disapproval written on Cousin Carlos's face resonates deep within me.

Something about Saul doesn't feel right. It pleases me to see that I'm not the only one picking up on a bad vibe from him.

Even the lurking black cat has returned and is arching its back up high as it snoops in the tree.

'He'll reveal his true self. Time will surely tell.'

"Youth Pastor, huh." Carlos scoffs. "*You'n from round 'ya* boy? *Is ya? Talkin' 'bout he* a Youth Pastor."

Tamara and Saul put their flirtation on pause while the old version of Carlos rears its ugly head, humiliating them with joke after joke like he'd win a prize for playing *the dozens*. The Roaster. The Comedian. The Shit Talker himself carried on far too long for Tamara's liking. Anytime Carlos cracks jokes and uses our Gullah dialect with heavy emphasis on specific words, it's time to put the moonshine mason jars back in the shed and call it a night.

Our kin enjoy a laugh at the newcomer's expense. I make myself visible in the window to be a part of the cypher, and search for the black cat wondering if it has lowered the arch in its back. I hate when cats do that, but it's one of those things you keep looking at no matter how much it disgusts you.

Thankfully, when I spot it hiding on the edge of a branch too thin to hold him, he sits in cat pose with a relaxed look on its face like it might have a contact high. If I didn't know any better, it's laughing along with us. Understands our humor. Listening with intent.

Popcorn pushes the chair next to him up a few spaces. "Have a seat." He tells Saul. "Tell us what you 'gon teach the youth 'bout the Lord."

"Nah, man. I'm good. I can tell you folk are clowning me. Y'all take it easy though."

Popcorn rests his arm on the back of the vacant chair. "That's what I thought."

Tamara throws up her fist to Carlos and Popcorn, then trails behind Saul like a puppy. I shake my head at her desperation when a sharp pinch startles me in my chest. The feeling alerts me to shift my eyes at Tam and Saul walking away. He's looking at me from the corner of his leering, evil eyes.

The look sends chills down my spine, but I didn't shy away. I stare back at him and hold his gaze for as long as he can stand it. He finally blinks and turns his head when he and Tamara pass by the window.

They sit on the back of Granddaddy's truck in the front yard. Too far for me to eavesdrop. Backs turned so I can't read their lips.

'Be smart, Tam. Don't fall for whatever he and the pastor came over here to sell.'

I reacquaint myself with the pages. Occasionally, I laugh at Carlos and the gang trading jokes and lose my place in the story. I find my way back where I left off for a few more minutes, then place a bookmark in the crease when Popcorn starts talking about a guy he went to school with named Dead Eye.

The name makes me think of Saul's evil eyes staring at me without my sister knowing. Eyes are the gateway to the soul. And his soul feels uneasy to me.

Carlos asks, "*Why they* call him Dead Eye?"

"Cause that motherfucker looked dead in the eyes. *Why you* think? His mama was known to work dark magic. Rumor was that magic was how he was born *wit' dem* dead ass eyes of his."

"Now I have seen, heard, and done some shit, but *whatchu mean by* he was born from dark magic?"

"When *dem* old ladies used to sit out in the park and weave their baskets down on Hester, I used to listen to them talk waiting for my turn to play ball. I heard one *of'em* say his mama and his daddy both worked dark voudon. His mama was barren and well—Dead Eye's old man was a rolling stone 'round town. They said the ladies all over town was in love wit' him, but scared of him at the same time. *Dem* old ladies called him the best looking dark skinned man they ever seen."

"That's cause they *ain't seen* me." Reno pops his collar.

The lot of them laugh, as do I standing in the window. Carlos and Popcorn toss empty cups at Reno. He swats at them and dodges the leftover spills of beer staining his clothes.

"Man you wish." Carlos fans him off. "Popcorn, you were saying."

Popcorn wets his throat with moonshine, and shrivels his lips as the burn eases down his chest. "Apparently, Dead Eye's old man took up with one young gal who put that good juju *on'em, 'cause he ain't leave* her like he did the rest. Mr. In and Out stayed out if you catch my drift. Dead Eye's mama wasn't having that. Whatever dark magic she was practicing before was nothing compared to what she did when she popped up pregnant, and got her husband back. Well, when the boy was born with the funny looking eyes, the old man wanted out. What he didn't know was it would cost him. He went back to that young gal and left his family for a good couple of months, then all of a sudden dropped dead in the street. That same day, the young gal he took up with found a line of pennies covered in white powder with the head side facing up at the threshold of her door. She called her neighbors over and all of them ran away. That gal didn't leave the house for days, and when her family came to check on her, she was dead. No cause of death found. No foul play."

"Shit, that boy *got a reason* to look dead in the eyes," says Reno.

I shake off Popcorn's chilling story, hoping to never cross the man with the dead eyes, and follow my instincts to pull my sister away from the man with evil in his. I've never seen her smile so big, or react like this to someone so fast. She's *cheese eating* like a rat in paradise. I can count all of her teeth *waaaay* from the porch.

I lie. "Tam, we gotta clean up the kitchen before Ma gets back."

"Can you do it without me this one time. Please?"

Saul looks back at me and grins. Tam can't see his eyes glistening, and not in a good way. I stare into them to enter his soul and gasp at the emptiness I see inside.

Holding my chest I say to her, "I'll do it this one time."

She mouths thank you and I go back inside. But not to clean up. I sneak through the back door and quietly creep to the side of the house. Protected by shadows provided from the position of the half moon.

Saul fills my sister's head with sweet pipe dreams. Lies upon lies about himself, and his intentions. I silently suck my teeth that Tam is taking him at his word.

Right on time, Ma, Uncle Wayne, and Aunt Sharon return. Tamara's body stiffens when she recognizes the lights of Ma's truck shining on her and her fraud friend. The three amigos roll up on them and look like triplets when they stare Saul up and down.

"Who is this knucklehead?" Uncle Wayne asks.

Tam's voice cracks with every syllable. "The new Youth Pastor at the church. Pastor Moore's brother."

Ma flails her hand. "Un-uh. Get in the house."

I race back inside through the back door and reposition myself in Granddaddy's chair. I overhear Ma asking Gran about my whereabouts. I pose with the book before she peeks her head in to put eyes on me.

"Come on. Let's get ready to go home," she says.

"Yes, ma'am."

"What you know 'bout that boy that got your sister acting all loose?"

I shrug. "The pastor's brother is all I know."

She sucks her teeth and sighs. "Umph. Well, let's get to moving."

The bookmark falls into the side of the chair. I grab the first thing I see from the dresser to mark my page. A tarnished ring with the yin and yang symbol serves in its place until I return, then I follow Ma's voice asking Pastor Moore a million questions about his brother.

The pastor recognizes the tone in my mother's third degree "Whew. Look at the time. Mrs. Sherman, you call me with whatever you need. The church is here for you and your family.".

Aunt Sharon answers for Gran. "We thank you."

The pastor tips his hat and shakes Gran's hand one final time. The television suddenly grows louder and creates a collective shift in the room at the words running on the chyron: **BREAKING NEWS.**

CHAPTER 22
GINA'S GRIEF

BREAKING NEWS: Body of Missing Girl Found

My mother's vision plays out on the television. The missing girl is reported as found, and the broadcast shares images of a pile of logs grouped together in the Ashley River. Emphasis on a red and white boat stands out in the background, and a helicopter flies across the screen before a man wearing a red shirt comes into frame to talk to the authorities.

"I was taking my son outchea for a ride and he asked, "Dad what is that over there?" I looked near the pack of logs and saw a high heel shoe poking out from the edge. I took my son home and came back out here hoping my eyes were deceiving me, but true enough there lied a body. I called the sheriff's office and stayed out here to show them where I saw it. It's unimaginable. I tell ya, I don't know what I'm gon' tell my son. But if it weren't for his young eyes, the body might have been ova dey for who knows how long. Just a terrible situation all 'round."

"That poor girl," says Pastor Moore. "Guess I better stop over there and see how the family is doing. You all have a good night."

Tear drops form in Ma's eyes. Her emotions radiate from her body in invisible waves, but are felt as everyone turns in her direction. One tear falls down her cheek. She exhales and wipes her face, but more fall when Uncle Junie rubs her shoulder.

Aunt Sharon hugs her from the other side. "We are what we are, Sis. You can't help it if your vision was right this time."

"I'm gonna call it for today. Girls, let's get ready to go." Ma hugs Uncle Junie and Aunt Sharon. "Mama, is there anything you need us to do before we leave?"

Gran nods. "There is something. You, Sharon, and the girls come down to my room. Wayne, see to it that everybody goes home. I'm *'bout* tired of all that partying in my yard. They *ain't gon* 'be nowhere to be found the day after the funeral no how."

"Yes, ma'am. I'll run everybody off, but you know the usual *suspects'll* be out back wit' me anyhow."

Gran grunts and limps on her right leg as she leads us down the hallway to her bedroom. She gets comfortable in her old red velvet covered chair, and lifts her leg on the stool. "Pass me my heating pad," she says, holding out her hands.

Tam grabs the pad from the night stand and plugs it into the wall. She lays it across Gran's knee, then props up her back pillow while she squirms in her chair, searching for her special spot.

"Now, I don't *wanna* hear no fuss with what I'm 'bout to say. Y'all know when one person in a marriage dies, sometimes it *ain't* long before the other one follows. Now, I don't plan on going *nowhere no* time soon, but I *ain't* the one in control. So, just in case what I say turns out to be true, I wanna have this talk over and done with."

"Mama, maybe you should rest and we talk ab..."

"Shhh. Didn't I say I don't wanna hear no fuss, *chile*?" Gran takes a deep breath. "Since you was a *chile* you been head-strong. Don't hear nothin' nobody got to say. This time be quiet and listen. I want the four of y'all to promise to always be there for one another." Gran points to Ma and Auntie. "You two do pretty good with each other. I'm proud *of the both of ya*."

"Gina knows I'll always stand in her corner." Aunt Sharon bumps her hips.

Gran points to me and Tamara."You two need to follow their lead."

I smile at Tamara. "I'll always look out for my sister."

"And Tamara baby. It *ain't* nothing wrong wit' smoking your weed. I mean you're young and sometimes it feels disrespectful, but I know your heart. Just promise me you'll be careful, and don't *never* smoke nothing that you didn't see get rolled—Or drink nothing you ain't poured yourself. And if you can, smoke at home and not in the street."

Tamara buries her face in her palms. "Yes, ma'am."

"One more thing. Before y'all leave I want y'all to go through my jewelry and take what you want. Don't want y'all fighting over nonsense after I'm gone like Mabel's bunch."

"You heard about that?" Aunt Sharon asks.

"Um hmm." Gran hums. "*Ain't* been dead a day and they already *done fell out* over who is getting what. Makes you wonder if ya family really loves ya. Even your own *chirrin*."

Aunt Sharon and Ma laugh, telling us how fast they were in and out of Mabel's house when they dropped off the flowers.

"We might have wasted our money taking those flowers over there," Ma says.

"I'd be surprised if they ever make it to water and not spread out on the floor!" Aunt Sharon cackles.

Gran shakes her head. "*Gon'* tear the house up before one *of'em* even *put dey* name on the deed."

Ma leers over to Tamara trying on earrings and smiling to herself in the mirror. She inhales a deep breath, then stares at me. I raise my brows and keep quiet, skimming through other items Gran has in her dresser drawers.

Colorful see-thru neck scarves, silver hair pins, and a gold box with a gold pen set inside by a company called Pierre Cardin are neatly stacked in boxes. I raise them one by one for Gran to see.

She beams. "They're yours."

I shimmy my shoulders and set them aside in the pile of items I want to keep.

Gran watches Tam pin another earring set to her ear. "You like those?"

"Yes, ma'am."

"You think that *boy'il like'm*?" Gran stares at the back of Tamara's head. "We see you smiling over there."

Tamara's cheeks rise higher than the moon in the sky.

Gran asks Ma. "I haven't had the talk with them. Have you?"

"They know what not to do, if that's what you mean."

"Well, Van and Tam, *I'm a* tell you girls like I told these two. You only got one time to slip up, and your life will no longer belong to *ya*. Don't fall for *'dem* sweet nothings *'lil* pissed tail boys will tell ya. They only care 'bout themselves. Most *of'em* anyhow. If there's one thing you remember me by, let it be this. My mama told me something and it turned out to be true. Sinners go to church and shout just like the saved, the devil can preach, and oftentimes he is good looking."

I chortle to myself at Gran's words of wisdom, but I worry Tam isn't taking the warning seriously. Gran's advice told me she was well aware of trouble looming, and didn't care for Saul because of her discernment. Unfortunately, the look on Tam's face says it's *gonna* take a lot more than a warning from the woman who's seen it all before our time to steer her away from the youth pastor.

'God help us.'

CHAPTER 23
SNEAKY SERPENTS

The house is far from quiet when I'm done with my shower. Tamara lies on her side of the bed smiling like a Cheshire Cat with her phone in her hand.

"What was all that preachin' coming from Gran?" she asks.

"You know exactly what she was getting at, and I agree with her. Something ain't right about that Saul. You were too busy grinning in his face to notice the red flags."

She scoffs. "So one day Gran tells us not to judge, but here she is judging. And you, too."

"Call it what you want. We're looking out for our own, and I'm telling you he ain't right behind his eyes. Look how easy he's put you in a trance."

Tamara lets me have the last word. She turns her back to me and sighs herself to sleep. I fall off sometime later with a racing mind hoping to pinpoint what it is about Saul that makes me uneasy. Searching for that answer doesn't come by the time the sun starts to rise.

The other side of the bed is empty and cold when I open my

eyes. The smell of cinnamon rolls float through the walls. I quickly jump up to make sure I get one before Ma packs them up.

Zu, Uncle Junie's wife—Well, Aunt Zu, sits at the breakfast table feeding her two year old when I stroll into the kitchen. The newborn sits in her lap sucking a bottle. She multitasks effortlessly.

"Good morning."

"Good morning. Your mother and Junie are both running errands this morning. Regina didn't want to wake you girls and left you here with me. Your sister's grabbing my charger from the car."

Tamara returns and places the charger on the counter. "You call Gran?" she asks me.

Zu pops her lips. "Oh, that's right. Your Gran said for one of you to call her when you woke up. I told Tamara and forgot to tell you just that quick."

I grab a warm roll from the tray and return to my room. With a mouth full of dough and icing clinging to my teeth, I smack in Gran's ear when she answers.

"It must be nice to sleep late."

"Sorry, Gran. Good morning."

"Morning *done come and gone*. Anyhow, you and your sister get over to the church before it gets too hot. I can't get an answer on their line and I narrowed down the songs I want the choir to sing. Get a pen and paper."

I chuckle at her stubborn ways and refusal to step out of her era, and pretend to write down the songs as I type them in a text to myself.

"I'm ready," I say.

"Tell Franny I only want two solos. I want 'When Sunday Comes', and 'The Battle Is The Lord's'. And during the benediction I want the choir to sing the chorus of 'Come On in the Room'. You got that?"

"Yes, ma'am. We'll take care of it right now."

I call the church and get the same results as Gran. I try a second time and still get no answer. I change out of my pajamas and dress in a tank and some shorts to withstand the heat for the mile walk. I grab Tamara and two waters from the kitchen, tell Aunt Zu what we're going, and head out of the door.

Tam is still salty with me for my brash words about her wannabe boyfriend. Her steps drag behind me, outside of the road line one too many times.

"Don't text and walk." I tease her. She ignores me. "The cinnamon rolls tasted different this morning. Who made them?"

"Uncle Junie's wife, I mean Aunt Zu did."

"She made'em how I like'em—Soft and gooey. Don't tell Ma she might have some competition."

"Umph." Tam grunts.

"Go on. Say *whatchu* holdin' back. Now ain't the time for you and me to be falling out."

"There's nothing to say."

But there is something to say, and Tamara is going to hold her grudge against me until she needs something...Like always.

As her steps guide her over the yellow line again, I slow my pace and walk beside her. She speeds up. I speed up. She slows down. I slow down.

"I'm gonna have to change shirts when we get back home. Look at me." I point to the sweat stain forming under the crease of my shirt.

"It's that new secretary's fault. I bet she's yapping on the line and not answering Gran's call."

"You're probably right."

Thumping beats pound from the bass of a car rolling up behind us. I place my hand across the front of Tam, and we stop to let the car pass. The tires screech and the brake lights flash as the driver slows down and blocks our path.

"If that's the green man, we're fucked," says Tam.

"If that was him I would have yelled run by now. That's Ricky's mama's car."

Tamara exhales and slides her bottle of water across her forehead. "Thank God."

Ricky waves from the car. "It's too hot to be walking out here. Hop in. I'll give y'all a lift."

"We're fine. You go ahead."

"The hell we are," says Tamara, then hops in the back seat.

I sigh and climb in after her. "We're just heading to the church. This really isn't necessary."

Ricky turns up the A.C. "You feel that. Yeah. You know y'all don't need to be walking out here."

The air conditioner blowing in my face feels like heaven. My shoulders relax from the cool sensation. My eyes close with relief to be out of the sun's oven. Ricky blasts his music and nods his head during the short drive, sneaking swift smiles my way.

He pulls into the church parking lot and turns down the volume. "I'm sorry about y'alls Grandpop."

"Thank you."

"Seemed like a real cool dude."

"He was." I open the door. "Thanks for the lift."

"How long are y'all gonna be. I'm making a quick run around the corner. I can take y'all back home. Won't be a problem."

"We won't be long and would love it if you could take us home." Tamara answers as she hops from the backseat.

"Cool, I'll swing back by."

As Ricky drives off, I nudge Tamara in the back of her head. "Why did you do that? I don't need him following us over to Gran's house giving our cousins a new punching bag."

"You came up with that from a car ride? Get over yourself, Van. He's just being nice. *Whatchu* scared of? Getting caught kissing him or something." She laughs.

The choir rehearsing lights up the entrance hall when we walk inside. Since we were toddlers, we were trained not to open the doors of the sanctuary while in session, so we wait until the song ends, then enter.

Franny's eyes lit at the sight of Tamara. "Hey, Tam. God sure does answer prayers. I heard you were finally going to sing with us. I have just the solo in mind." Franny waves for her to come forward.

Tam's eyes bulge from her head, while her tongue ties itself in knots. A low murmur sounds from her throat that I'm sure is a cuss word, and she stands still and utters, "Help me out here."

"Ms. Franny, we have errands to run together and just stopped by because our Gran has been calling all morning to give you the list of songs for the funeral. Since no one answered, she told us to come tell you in person."

She sighs. "That's what happens when you hire young people to do an adult's job. Let's see the list."

I pull out my phone and show her the text I sent to myself.

"Vanya, go to the office and write these songs down for me."

I roll my eyes. "Yes, ma'am."

"Tam, she can take care of that alone. I'd like to have a word with you."

I giggle as I leave Tamara bouncing a check her ass doesn't want to cash. I want to watch her wiggle her way out of saying she would think about joining the choir to impress Saul, so I hurry to the office to make the list.

I'm in the correct place to make a plan and watch God laugh, because he derails my front row seat to watch Tamara squirm. But the devil is busy as well, proving that when you say his name, or think of him, he too will appear. I find him right there in the office—Saul, smiling in the young secretary's face the same way he was smiling in my sister's face less than 24 hours ago.

She's as smitten as Tam, and not answering the phone.

I clear my throat. "I need pen and paper for Ms. Franny. Please."

Her eyes shoot at me like lasers when she hands me a square post-it and ink pen.

"Thank you." I roll my eyes and exit the office.

Near the hallway of the foyer, I stick the note to the wall and write down the songs. I look above the pad and see a shadow coming toward me. Saul's silhouette stands behind me tall, awkward, and silent.

I gasp. "Excuse me."

"A hello would be nice."

I return to the list.

"You don't talk much, do you?"

I shake my head side to side. "I need to get by please."

Saul blocks me each time I attempt to go around him. The same enchanting smile he was flashing for the secretary, he flashes for me. His dark eyes narrow while trying to gaze into mine. His shadow appears behind him and I see him clear his day. His aura is black as night and my heart beats fast from the energy bouncing off of him.

"Tam is inside with the choir if you wanna go say hi." I ease one foot past him.

"But I'm tryna talk to you."

The front door of the church swings open and I take a breath. My guardian angel walks in and I say internally, *'Yes! I am saved from this pulpit pimp.'*

Saul's eyes gleam. He wraps his arm around me. "Pretend you're my girlfriend."

"What?"

"My friend from back in the day just walked in. Tell him you're my girlfriend."

My back goes numb and my feet freeze as my hand struggles

to remove his from my shoulder. "Why would I lie for you? And in church? Some Youth Pastor you are." I snap, pricking the back of his hand with my fingernails.

Ricky's voice wobbles. "Everything alright?"

I stare at him with enlarged eyes begging for help, and shake my head side to side inconspicuously.

Saul's grip around my shoulder grows tighter. "What's up man? I was coming to holla at you. I'm here for good now."

Ricky looks at the horror on my face. "Oh yeah." He drags his words and raises his fist to give Saul a pound.

Saul awkwardly reciprocates with the wrong fist. "I want you to meet my girl."

I look back at Saul's hand on my shoulder, and prick him again with my sharpest nail. "Stop lying. You don't even know my name."

Ricky laughs. "It's good you're back in town, man." He snickers and smiles at me. "You ready?"

"Yeah. Let me give this to Ms. Franny and grab my sister."

Saul's grip quickly loosens. Ricky and I look into each other's eyes and turn to enter the sanctuary.

"What was that about?" he whispers.

"I have no idea. Thank God you came in when you did."

Tamara sits in the first row near the usher's double door entrance. A tear falls from her right eye as I walk past her before she takes the stage. She refuses to make eye contact with me. Suddenly, I don't want to watch her squirm anymore.

I pass the list to Ms. Franny. "Here's my grandmother's request. We've got to get going."

Ms. Franny pats me on the back and nods, then cues the choir to settle down for the next song. Tamara walks out without me, and Ricky and I find our way back outside in the heat.

"Now do you mind telling me what's up with you and my boy, Saul."

"Not a thing. He was cracking on Tam yesterday."

The heat nearly knocks me back inside.

"You glad I came back for you, *innit*?"

"Yes, Ricky. Grateful." I glance at the hood of his car. "What happened here?"

Tamara sneaks up on us. "I was 'bout to ask the same thing? I didn't see that when you picked us up."

Ricky opens the car door for me. "No wonder you two out here walking all free willy nilly. Y'all ain't heard the lizard man is on the loose."

CHAPTER 24
CREEK CHAOS

"Hell naw we ain't heard *nuttin' 'bout no* Lizard Man on the loose!" Tamara fusses. "By chance does he look like a little leprechaun running around?"

Ricky scowls. "Not even close. This thing is over six feet tall with a pointed head, long tail, and as you can see has stretched out claws." He points to the hood. "Why you asking 'bout a leprechaun?"

I cut in. "So, you saw this lizard man with your own two eyes?"

"Yeah, but I won't admit that to anyone else if I'm asked. I have a reputation to protect in these streets. Besides, according to my grandfather's scanner, the police have other people on record seeing it last night, so they don't need a statement from me."

Tamara and I circle Ricky's car and study the claw marks. They're long but resemble a bear or tiger's paw. The strikes curve and are cut deep into the steel. And the size of them is frightening.

I lean forward to catch a whiff of the mark. "The imprint

smells like the marsh. We need more details about this thing. Where did you see it? What did you do? Did it see you?"

"Whoa, whoa, whoa. Get in and I'll tell ya everything."

I hold my finger above the dented surface. "Hey Tam, what do you think will happen if I touch it?"

She rolls her eyes and gets in the car.

"What did I do to you?"

Ricky interrupts before she responds. "I wouldn't touch that if I were you."

"Why not?"

"That thing was ugly. I wouldn't trust it. My old man is looking for a new hood at the junkyard as we speak."

I pull my hand back and get in the car. Tamara talks to Ricky and ignores me during the short drive home. She doesn't hold back on the questions, and Ricky happily offers up all of the information he can share.

"I was parked down by Dead Man Creek handling some business last night when I saw it. I couldn't shake the feeling I was being watched, ya know. So, I looked up, and there it was staring at me."

"What color was it? Light green or dark green?" Tamara asks.

"I couldn't tell ya. It was dark. Plus, it was near the marsh so if it came from out of there it was covered in mud. I know it had yellow eyes."

"So when you saw it staring at you what did you do?"

"I blew the horn, thinking it was some jokey, lame ass dude in a costume, but it didn't like that loud noise. *I'on* know if it spooked him or what, but that shit knocked my mama's car back, then jumped on the hood. I got scared as hell when its nails started digging in the hood. I cranked up and left tire tracks in the road. If it fell off 'cause of how wild I took off, or jumped off on its own—I couldn't tell ya. All I know is *I'ne* look back."

"You scared to go back?"

"Would you go back?"

"I kind of wanna go down there now to see if you really left tire marks in the road."

"Is that what it will take for you to believe me?"

"Who says I don't believe you?"

"I heard they're gonna talk about it tonight on the news. Apparently, this isn't the first time someone has reported this thing, but the media and the cops have kept quiet about it for years."

"Years?" Tamara sucks her teeth. "It must have spooked some important rich person."

"That'll get'em talking," I add.

Tamara turns up her lips and talks over me. "Ricky, on a scale of one to ten, how scared were you?"

"A twelve! That shit was huge. Can you imagine a ugly ass lizard man staring you in the eyes, and knocking a car this heavy around like it was nothing?"

"Actually, I could."

Ricky serves me a questionable look. "You'd probably shit yourself."

"Did you shit yourself?" I ask him.

He and I laugh, then settle down when we notice Tamara's straight face. I stare at her until she makes eye contact with me.

"That was funny as hell," I say.

"To you."

"Why are you mad at me?"

Her face scrunches. "Don't act innocent. I saw what happened at the church."

Ricky turns the music all the way down.

"Ricky, you mind telling my sister what she saw, please?"

He adjusts the rearview mirror. "Van told me my old buddy was *tryna* get at you yesterday. She was having a hard time getting him to leave her alone...Even after I walked in."

"I told you something about him wasn't right. Hell, I walked in on him and the young secretary flirting in the office. That's why she wasn't answering the phone. I know what kind of pastor he's gonna be."

Ricky chuckles. "Not the good kind." He looks at Tam in the mirror. "I don't normally speak on such matters, but Tam I like you. Trust me, don't get involved with him. That's all I'm gonna say."

Ricky considers himself to be cool and was the guy most of the boys at school got along with. It was out of character for him to weigh in on matters of the heart, but I'm glad he did because Tamara needed to hear Saul was bad news from someone other than me or Gran.

I smile at him. "Did I thank you?"

"I can't remember, but it's all love." He smiles back at me.

"Well, just in case I haven't said it, thank you. Now keep your eyes on the road, playboy. I know you weren't alone at Dead Man Creek last night."

Ricky's mouth twists to the side. His eyelids stretch until a line forms in the middle of his forehead, and his eyes dance with the lines in the middle of the road. He has the worst lying tell I've ever seen. He made the same face when he denied telling everyone about our make out session in the park.

"I gotta question. Why do you two believe my story so easily?"

Tam finally looks at me. "The world is full of wonders and creepy shit."

"Y'all really wanna go down there? To Dead Man Creek?"

Tam nods. We share a smirk, then I check the time. We have a little leeway to wiggle in a quick trip before Ma or Gran come looking for us.

"Yeah, but make it quick," I say.

Tamara and I ride super low on our way to Dead Man Creek

until we pass Gran's house. The last thing we need is to be seen in the car with a boy, or accused of joyriding with a boy. Ricky slows down when we're a quarter of a mile away, then the car comes to a sudden halt before the last street that merges with a sharp turn. The entrance melds with a muddy road that leads to the creek.

"Why have we stopped?" Tamara asks.

"Traffic is backed up like a *mug*," says Ricky.

"Is it safe to sit up yet?" Tam complains. "My neck is getting a crook in it."

"Yeah, y'all should be straight. Scared asses." Ricky chuckles.

The road is crowded yards away before the final turn. People are parking their cars on the side of the road, heading for the creek on foot.

"Before either of you suggest it, I'm not getting out of this car," he says.

Tam cuts him off. "You ain't gotta worry about us saying *nuttin' like dat*. In fact, you can turn the car around. If we wait in this jam, we're gonna get in trouble."

A split second after Tamara mentions we need to leave, Ricky's radio changes the channel on its own, and the volume turns up to full blast. He reaches for the dial while Tam and I cover our ears.

"What the hell?" he says, turning down the volume and switching the setting back to his playlist. "I don't know why it did that. That's never happened before." He stares at me. "Freaky."

"Maybe you should try to wiggle us out of here and take us home," I say, listening to the voice Aunt Sharon told me to follow.

Ricky three point turns in the middle of the road. While we wait in traffic to make it back to the main road, a few of our classmates spot us and walk over to the car.

"Did y'all make it into the creek?" Ricky asks Black.

"Yup. It's a circus back there. Cameras and reporters are everywhere. Some of us are coming back tonight when the crowd dies down."

Ricky shakes his head. "Y'all crazy for that man."

"Maybe, but we're coming strapped. If that *sonbitch* come at me I'm putting him down *fasho*."

"That little .38 you carry ain't *gon* do nothin' to that thing, man." Ricky cackles. "But y'all be easy out there tonight. Ya won't see me."

Tam and I share a look. We don't have to say it aloud. We are thinking the same thought about Ricky's wavering voice and vibe.

'*That lizard spooked the hell out of Ricky.*'

The car behind us blows their horn. Ricky and Black wrap up their conversation and bump fists, then speeds off to get us home. He comes inside to offer his condolences. He may have a big mouth, but he is respectful and mannerable with the elders.

When he leaves, we go outside and speak to Popcorn sitting under the shade of the angel oak tree in the backyard.

"Who was that clown?" Popcorn asks.

"Vanya's boyfriend."

"Boyfriend? The bookworm got a boyfriend? When? How? And what were y'all doing in the car with him?"

I reverse the line of questioning. "What are you doing over here so early? And why are you sitting out here in this heat?"

"I'm not staying out here long. Wayne and Junie asked me to sit tight until they return. You know. Make sure everything is cool and calm as more people are expected to pop in closer to the day of the funeral."

I sigh. "Two more days of the circus."

"You got that right. Then you have to worry about the quiet."

CHAPTER 25
LOADED LESSONS

As the heat scorches everything outside, Tamara and I finish off a list of chores Gran gave us to complete before the next horde pours in. When no one is looking, I do a deodorant check. The few visitors are already raising the temperature in the house. Ma and Aunt Sharon finally arrive and I pray one of them has the wits to run some of them off.

Ma calls on me. "Vanya, go tell your uncles I said to stop bickering, and bring in the rest of the bags before something spoils."

"Yes, ma'am."

Tamara unloads the first bag Aunt Sharon places on the table. "Ma, did y'all hear about what happened down at the creek?"

"Yeah, we heard. Come help me lay these clothes out on the bed for Mama to try on."

I brace myself to be smacked by dry heat. The bright sun shines directly on top of the porch steps, sizzling me like a fajita, but I still make my way over to the truck where Uncle Wayne and Uncle Junie are nearly at blows.

Their heated debate consists of materialism and favoritism. Who should get what of Granddaddy's belongings not specified in his will. Who deserved his coin collection, who should have his expensive hats and shoes. Who was he the most proud of, and which one of them he loved more.

I'm melting, waiting for the right time to chime in with Ma's demand. Eventually, I chicken out and grab Popcorn to break the two of them up.

Granddaddy's cool room and lounge chair is the best hiding place to be away from the drama, the arguments, the countless speculations if the lizard man is real or a hoax, and the egos selecting which dress and jewelry set Gran should wear to the funeral. I ball up into a knot and dive back into my book.

"Now that feels good!" Uncle Wayne shouts outside my window.

I've made good progress to the middle of the novel, but I have to see what the commotion is all about in the backyard. If curiosity kills cats, consider myself slain.

I prop my head high enough above the window and spot a new addition to the family circle. An industrial sized cooling fan blows beside the tables and chairs under the tree. Uncle Wayne's thick afro doesn't move when he stands in front of it, but the stringy strands in Popcorn's beard slightly wiggle from the strong breeze.

"Mama is gonna kill you when she sees this!" Uncle Junie fusses.

"You enjoying it, too, *ain't cha*?"

Uncle Junie fans him off.

Uncle Wayne sips from a beer can. "That's what I thought. I pay Mama's light bill anyway. You don't do nothin' but judge and complain."

Popcorn paces back and forth. "We should have thought of this a long time ago."

Uncle Wayne taps his temple. "Better late than never."

Cousin Reno arrives and the chatter out back grows louder. I finish my book and join them when the sun turns orange in the sky, and the humidity takes its chill pill for the evening.

"Did y'all know bookworm had a boyfriend?" Popcorn rats me out.

My uncles and cousins turn silent and stare at me like I'm a leper of some kind.

"Where is he?" Uncle Wayne asks.

"The boy Popcorn is referring to is my friend…Not my boyfriend. And I don't know where he is. He might be down at the creek with his friends shooting at that lizard."

"Shooting what? Spitballs?" Reno cackles, holding his stomach.

The lot of my cousins and uncles bray at Reno's funny remark. Each one of them adds a random spin to his quip such as shooting darts, shooting blanks, and shooting stars.

"Ha ha ha very funny mutha…" I stop short of the famous line.

"Whoa. Whoa. Whoa Little Eddie. Somebody get my niece a shiny, red leather suit and a comedy special." Uncle Wayne keels over laughing. "Leave it up to the smart one to remember something I should've never let her watch."

"For your friends sake, I hope they know what they're doing. Ain't no telling what's in the swamp as many hurricanes *done passed* through here," Reno adds.

Uncle Wayne nods. "Now you ain't telling one lie there."

I step in front of the fan. "I was worried it's more than one of them and the others are hiding in the woods."

My comment is met with a collective silence. Reno lifts the hem of his t-shirt. He raises his brows as he reveals a gun tucked by his waist.

"If anything come out dem there woods it'll die in this back-yard," he says.

Uncle Wayne moans. "It'll be met with more than that pellet gun." He laughs and the rest follow. "I'm glad you and your sister had enough sense not to join your idiot friends. But it does raise the question. Do you and your sister know how to shoot?"

"No, sir."

"Sir?" Uncle Wayne chuckles. "Reno, what say we take the girls down to the creek with the rest of the fools and show them how to shoot?"

"Just 'cause I carry a gun don't mean I go looking for a gun fight— But we should teach them how to shoot. Go get your sister. We have a couple of ground rules to go over first."

I run inside to find Tamara with a vivid image of my mother's face when she was shooting at that devil figure the other night. The fearless look in her eyes under the candlelit sky, and the power she displayed while defending us is something I wish I possessed. And now that a lesson about gunfire is being offered, I'm all for learning to load, cock, and shoot.

The kitchen is packed and Tamara is nowhere in sight. I come up empty in the living room also. Gran gives me a look for being short with those offering their condolences.

I pad past her and speed down the hallway. I turn the knob to our bedroom, then pause before I push it open. A screeching sound rings in my ears. Tamara sits in front of the mirror doing silly girl magic. I cover my mouth, holding in my laughter as I watch her tape a piece of paper beneath her bra through the slim crack in the door.

She flinches as I invade her privacy. "Uncle Wayne and Reno want to teach us how to shoot a gun. Come outside."

"Okay."

"Tamara, tell me you didn't do what I think you did?"

"I have no idea what you're..."

I cut her off. "The paper taped under your bra. Please tell me you didn't put that pulpit pimp's name next to your heart after what happened today."

"So what if I did?"

"Take it off before it really works and you're stuck being in love with that loser. Can you honestly think the first boy you like who flirts with everyone, and lies to you, is worth ending up like one of the stories Aunt Sharon and Uncle Wayne told us about?"

"Easy for you to say. You've had two boys pining for you today."

"Take notes. Soulless Saul was about to kiss the secretary when I walked in the office. He and Ricky are childhood friends. When he saw him come into the church, he asked me to lie and tell Ricky I was his girlfriend to one up him and I refused. The boy is a player who likes to play games. And also a liar because he lied to Ricky for no reason at all. We laughed at him in his face and left him standing there like a dufus. And here you are channeling for him to be some great love of your life. Take that shit off of you and come outside."

Tamara's eyes water as she rips the translucent tape from her skin.

I hug her. "Your great love is probably waiting on you when you get to college. Now, let's go outside and be with the people who really love us." I create a small flame on the tip of my index finger. "Burn it."

Tamara looks at me with fear and delusion. She raises the love plea paper slowly, folds it in half, then drops it into the fire. As she backs away from me, her eyes remain fixated on the paper until it vanishes into the air.

"So, this is you now? Doing magic tricks from your fingertips?"

"It's my gift, so this is me. There's no telling what yours was, but you renounced it. Do you regret doing that?"

"Un-uh. I still want no part of that."

I ball my hand into a fist and put out the flame. Tamara reaches for my hand and examines my fingers, tracing them with hers.

She grunts. "They're warm, but no trace of fire, or burn marks anywhere. How is that possible?"

"I don't know. I didn't have any marks after the first time either."

"And you can withstand the heat with no problem?"

"So far I haven't experienced any."

"What does it feel like?" She grabs my hands and inspects them closer than the first time.

"Like a minor itch on the tips of my fingers, and a heaviness in my chest. I haven't had anyone to teach me anything about my gift, but my mind tells me the heavy feeling is where I draw my power from, and serves as a guide to not abuse it. And I won't. Great-Great-Great-Gran told me to keep this gift a secret. I trust you will."

Tamara zips her lips shut with her finger. "My lips are sealed."

"She also told me she can summon rain. I have a feeling that would have been your gift, but we'll never know. Will we?"

The door flies open.

Tamara gasps. "Jesus."

"Why are you two hiding in here?" Ma asks, with Aunt Sharon on her heels.

"We're on our way outside. Uncle Wayne and Cousin Reno are about to teach us how to shoot."

Ma's brows curve. "I suppose that's fine. But first, your aunt and I have something to tell you. I don't know how you knew what you told us, but it was true."

Aunt Sharon digs into her purse and turns a yellow envelope

upside down. Granddaddy's watch falls into her hands. She smiles at me then extends her hand to Tamara.

"Daddy wanted you to have this." She fastens the watch on her wrist. "He was never mad at you. He just wanted you to learn a lesson."

Tamara stutters. "But I..."

"He left instructions on where to find it, and who to give it to...You."

Tears well in Tamara's eyes. It takes a minute, but they form puddles in all four corners. Months of anguish disappear from her spirit. In this moment she accepts that she is forgiven and she is loved. Not the desperate person she was channeling moments ago.

"Know your worth. Know you're worthy of real love. Know that you already have it with us," I say. "Now let's go pop some smoke."

"Listen to you." Ma snaps. "You're a little too eager to click clack pull a wig back. I may need to rethink this."

"After the week we've had, and news of a Lizard Man on the loose, me and Tam need lessons to take care of ourselves like you and Aunt Sharon."

Ma sighs. "Hurry up. We're going home in an hour."

Aunt Sharon steps aside to let us pass. "This *oughta* be good."

CHAPTER 26

CLICK CLACK

Uncle Wayne and Popcorn line up the wooden keg and metal garbage cans in a row on the side of the shed. The moonlight illuminates the field. A beautiful picture that a painter would love to capture on a canvas is about to receive empty shells as we're trained for violence. I save the image in my head, then prepare to temporarily desecrate it.

In the center of each stand, Uncle Wayne places empty beer cans and bottles across the top. Aunt Sharon joins us with her Smith & Wesson across her shoulder. Ma grabs one of Granddaddy's shotguns from the shed and lines up next to her.

The crickets, katydids, and cicadas chirp and buzz louder than I've heard in weeks after Popcorn lowers the music.

He unplugs the whirring fan. "Almost ready?!"

Uncle Wayne shouts. "Just about."

Uncle Reno pulls his gun from his holster. "Now before we shoot, you girls need to learn lesson one. You don't pull out your piece unless you're gonna use it. And if you're gonna use it, you best have good aim. Got it?"

"Got it."

"Lesson two. Never point this end towards yourself." His fingers run up and down the barrel.

"That's self-explanatory," says Tamara.

Uncle Reno sighs. "You would think so, but accidents happen. Now, no more sassing. Pay attention. Always make sure your safety is on until it's time to use your weapon."

Uncle Wayne yells. "Alright! Let's get ready for round one!"

"Now girls, I promise to take you down to the range one day, but for now target practice is gon' be hittin' those cans and bottles. Carlos, give Vanya your piece." Reno passes Tamara his thirty-eight special. "Hold it like this."

Carlos stands up. "What makes you think I have my gun on me?"

"The day a gangster doesn't carry is the day water is no longer wet. Hand it over."

Carlos lifts his shirt, reaches around his waist, and turns the gun towards the ground as it hangs from the guard.

"Y'all see how he handles that beauty." Reno jokes. "Ain't nobody out here thought for a second you wasn't holding, cous."

Carlos drops his head and laughs along with everyone out back. Aunt Sharon and Ma raise their rifles when the joke dies down. They aim their weapons toward our targets twenty-five feet down the field.

Ma's voice sounds muffled against her shirt when she says, "Thank y'all for letting my girls hold your straps, 'cause the kickback from these rifles would be a little too much for them."

"Girls, *ya see* how poised your mother and Sharon are standing. They can't teach that grace in ballet school. That's the Sherman lessons inbred *in'em*. Now emulate their stance," Reno instructs.

Tam and I raise our arms and copy the way Ma and Aunt

Sharon are standing—Still, arms straight with a minor bend at the elbow, back straight, and focused.

"Next, remove your safety and adjust your sight. Cock your hammer. Become one with your target, and be sure you hold steady. When I call your name, pull the trigger and take your shot. Sharon!" Reno calls.

Boom! Her rifle sounds off.

"Vanya!"

Pow! The bullet shoots from my pistol.

"Tam!"

Pap! Pap! Crack!

"Cheater! I said take one shot!"

Bang!

"I didn't call your name, Gina!"

"You were taking too long."

"Safety's on!" Reno pats Tamara and I on the shoulder.

A few shouts and a round of applause fills the backyard. I look over my shoulder and see Gran is watching us from behind the sheers in the living room.

"From here it looks like everyone hit their target except for Vanya. I believe you grazed the tip of the can on your target. I could have sworn I heard a *ting* on your round," says Reno.

"I'll go see," I say, then walk towards the field.

"Ah hell," says Uncle Wayne. "Don't look now, but that pesky cat is back up there in the tree watching us."

"Whichever one of y'all has Carlos's gun should shoot at his creepy ass," says Popcorn.

"That would be me!" I yell.

Uncle Wayne holds up his hands. "Naw. The only animal we shoot is deer 'round these parts."

"I didn't say kill it. I said shoot at it. Scare it away."

I study my can, noticing a chip missing from the pop tab. Up close, I point my gun at the can and shoot it off of the keg. My family turns quiet and looks at me in unison.

"Well that's another way to skin a cat," says Carlos.

My family laughs at his quip.

Carlos then hops up from his chair. "I'll be inside. Let me know when y'all are done with my heat."

Ma points for Uncle Wayne to set up more cans and bottles. "Two more rounds, girls, then we're calling it a night." She winks at Aunt Sharon. "Move'm further back! I got twenty-twenty baby!"

Aunt Sharon clicks her tongue. "You ain't alone. I still got it, *Sistah*."

"We'll see about that."

During round two of target practice, I notice a difference in Tamara. The look of confusion and fear on her face resembles that of the night we were chased by the man with the shifting green and black face.

"You alright?" I ask her.

"No."

"Is the gunfire upsetting you?"

"No," she answers, then unloads multiple shots and clears the cans and bottles from her position.

"This *youngin'* is trigger happy," Reno whispers loud enough for us to hear. "Sharon!"

Bang! Bang! Pow! Boom! Plow! Bang! Ma shoots alongside Aunt Sharon and they clear the cans and bottles Tamara left on the podium.

"Just like her mother." Reno chuckles. "Good job, ladies. "I'll be happy to show y'all off down at the range." Reno collects the guns from me and Tamara, then squeezes both of our shoulders.

"Un, un, un," Ma kisses her teeth. "Give me those." She takes the guns from Reno's hand. "I don't need my girls mixed up in street shit. I'll be right back. You two follow me." She commands, leading us into the shed.

Inside she wipes off our fingerprints from the guns, and rubs her rifle down with alcohol. Then, she takes a cloth hanging on a nail near the door, and shines them with a cleaning solution and oil.

"You two did good out there. Your father and grandfather would be proud." She praises us with a distant glance and a curve formed on the side of her mouth. "Now promise me you won't pick up a gun unless your life depends on it. Only if you're in danger and feel threatened."

"We promise."

"I trust you two to make wise choices, like not going down to the creek with your lookin' for trouble friends."

Tamara and I look at Ma with widened pupils. The curve on the side of her mouth rises into a full blown smile. Her eyes dance with a know-it-all spirit. Her motherly dominance towers us like an invisible force field.

"Yeah, I know about it. So do most of the other parents. I'm glad I didn't have to drag you two from down there. Now take note. Daddy would have had my hide if he saw me wiping the outside of these heaters with alcohol, but I'm not taking any chances with those two fools. Ain't no telling how many bodies are on these, so I'm making sure your fingerprints are nowhere to be found on them. *Ya hear me*?"

"Yes, ma'am."

Ma hands Reno his gun with the cloth she used to clean it. "She's all shined up for ya. See you tomorrow at the wake."

We follow her inside to give Gran a kiss goodnight. On our way out, we run into Carlos sitting near the front door. Ma puts the white cloth covering his gun in his hand.

"This belongs to you. Thanks for letting my girl use it. We'll see you tomorrow."

"See y'all." Carlos lifts his shirt and places his weapon behind his back. He has the same disheveled look on his face as Tamara. "Good night," he adds, just before he leaves.

"I wonder what got into him?" Ma asks.

"The cat did," says Tamara.

"How do you know?"

"Because I heard what it said to him."

CHAPTER 27

SEEING SPIRITS

Ma's eyebrows damn near lift off her face. "You heard the cat speak?"

Tam nods. "When Vanya shot her target up close, Carlos said, "It's more than one way to skin a cat." The cat hopped down from the tree, looked at him and said, "You would know." He wasn't lying when he said they talk to him."

"That explains why he went in the house," I say.

Ma is in such shock she doesn't blink, but I'm overflowing with questions. What does this mean? Is communicating with nature Tam's gift? Was renouncing her gift done in vain? Can you disown what is tied to you through birth? Why couldn't the rest of us hear the cat speak? Does it talk to them telepathically? Or did it verbally have a conversation and magically mute its words from the rest of us?

Aunt Sharon blows through the front door like the wind and breaks our trance. "Everybody's phone is about to start going off. That lizard man thing just scared those crazy kids at Dead Man Creek. Someone called Popcorn and said they saw yellow eyes glowing in the cordgrass. They threw rocks at it and it lunged forward instead of moving back, so one of those crazy kids shot at it, and now they don't know where the thing is headed."

Ma snaps her fingers. "Tell Mama's company it's time for them to leave. We're headed home, too. You wanna stay with us tonight?"

Auntie snaps. "I ain't scared, but I will stay the night. Be over *in a short* with Junie and his bunch."

Ma pulls Uncle Wayne aside. "I oiled Granddaddy's gun. Mama can use some rest. Send everyone home and protect the house."

"No needn't worry 'bout us. I'll shoot the bastard if it steps on this land," he says.

The sentiment carries over into our house. Ma parks the truck in the garage, unlocks my father's cabinet, and brings his rifle and handgun inside.

"You two take your bath before the rest of them get here so the hot water can rebuild."

After Zu puts her babies to sleep, she joins us in the kitchen. She stands at the island counter passing snacks around, while Aunt Sharon, Uncle Junie and Ma entertain us with stories Gran passed down to them.

"You remember that time Mama came home from one of those houses she worked in, and told us she saw that old lady's spirit rise from her body when she died," says Uncle Junie.

Ma shivers. "Yeah, I remember that one. I didn't sleep for a week when she told us about the red devil tapping at Mrs. Wilcox's window before she died."

"Oh yeah, the mean lady. I couldn't get you out of my bed after that. It was longer than a week if I remember correctly." Aunt Sharon laughs out loud. "I never believed Mama's tales until I got older, and all the unexplainable things started happening before my very own eyes."

Uncle Junie puckers his lips. "Daddy only told us one tale. Well it was more like a warning. Remember when he said, "Don't ever drive down Archdale Street at night.""

Aunt Sharon confesses. "I do and I did. And it isn't a tale." She raises a brow. "Now, I didn't see what Daddy said was out there, but I saw something."

"What did your father say was out there?" Zu asks.

My mother, aunt, and uncle look at each other like guilty kids caught stealing candy, then burst into a tearful laughter. Zu, Tam, and I stare at them anxious to learn what was so funny, and why the tears.

Ma exhales. "Daddy said at night all of the buried dead could be seen in the graveyard, or walking down the road."

Junie adds, "he claimed he saw a man floating next to his car with no legs. The man never looked at him, but kept up with his car until he turned off the street. He convinced himself that what he saw wasn't real, so he took that same route home again, and vowed to never set foot on that road ever again when he saw a headless horseman."

Aunt Sharon bites on a chip. "Other people say they can see the dead standing in the graveyard some nights. Everybody I know avoids that street altogether because of the strange accounts and sightings people have reported."

Zu questions. "And you went down there anyway?"

"Well, I don't scare easily, so yeah I went one night."

"And?"

"I don't know what I saw. It wasn't see-through like most people describe ghosts. It was opaque and limping. From what I can remember, it had on torn, worn out funeral clothes, and it was standing with its back turned away from the road. I had to be driving 2 miles per hour. You know, tiptoeing my way through to make a full observation. Suddenly, it looked at me in a sinister fashion. My heart damn near jumped *outta* my chest. Then, it started running fast towards my car, so I mashed on the gas and burned rubber. I yielded at the stop sign at the end of Archdale and Queen, and got the hell out of dodge. Shit, I hit something in the road before I turned, too, but *I'ne* stop to see what, and *I'ne* been back since." Auntie crosses her chest with the four corners of the cross. "I drove so fast I could smell the tar from the road and the burning of my tires when I got home."

Zu says. "But what did you hit? It could have been a small child, or a dog."

"Then whoever let their child roam the street that time of night has more explaining to do than me. And if it was a dog, they all go to heaven, don't they?"

Tamara and I chuckle at Aunt Sharon setting Zu straight.

Aunt Sharon shakes her head. "Junie, I tell ya, you would marry one of "*them*" people."

Zu's hand rises to her hip. "What do you mean by one of "*them*" people?"

"The kind of people who care more about if the dog lived than the likes of me. I just said I was chased by a sinister entity, and you are asking about an imaginary dog. It could have been a pothole I hit for all I know. I wasn't going back to find out."

"Alright you two. Don't get started. We got a green thing-a-ma-jig on the loose. Let's hope they catch it or someone puts it down so we don't have to be held up in the house," says Ma.

My aunts settle their differences and Uncle Junie lightens the mood with memories of all the trouble they used to get into as kids. They tap their beers and shove each other as Tam and I sneak off and lock ourselves in our room.

Tamara plops down on the bed. "You talk to Ricky?"

"Not yet."

"I bet he knows who shot at that thing." She smiles. "I hope it bleeds to death."

"I hope we never see it."

"Me, too. I've seen enough."

Tamara buries her face in her palms so I can't see her cry. I listen to her silent sniffles and the trapped air in her chest from hiding her tears. When she finally sighs, a hard cry overcomes her.

I weep with her. "I believe you by the way. Do you wanna talk about it?"

"No." She murmurs. "I'm hoping I forget the whole thing."

I edge to the foot of the bed and hug my sister from behind, wishing I could take her fear and pain away. She holds onto my arm like a comfort pillow until she cries herself to sleep. I pull her up to her side of the bed, then think about Aunt Sharon's encounter on Archdale Street when my thoughts won't let me go to sleep. Something about her story doesn't sit well in my bones.

I have no way to prove what I suspect. I believe the spirit she saw that night is still with her, and was the coughing entity we heard in her basement. Now I have to find a way to tell her and hope to God she believes me.

CHAPTER 28
MERCY ME

It's the morning of the wake, and more distant relatives are expected to pour into Gran's house, especially with Mildred's sudden demise. Ma wakes us earlier than normal so we're at Gran's by nine o'clock. The driveway and yard is already half-full with car tags from in and out of state.

Uncle Junie and Aunt Sharon beat us there, and have aligned the big table with two foldable tables from the shed. She's set the food in a buffet style for the expected crowd. Uncle Junie fills the aluminum trays with pancakes, scrambled eggs, grits, and sausages. He stirs shredded cheese into the last pot of grits steaming on the stove. Once it's blended, Auntie lifts the top so he can pour them in the pan. Tam and I grab a plate of every-thing then escape into Granddad's room before we're put to work.

She stretches across the bed, still sleepy as am I. I ball up beneath a blanket in my favorite chair, finish my food and close my eyes.

Tamara turns her back to me. "I'm gonna take a nap. If Ma

finds us, please beg her to let me sleep. I didn't sleep too well last night."

"That's a lie. You fell asleep in my arms. I had to drag your butt to your side of the bed."

"I had a bad dream and woke up at two o'clock. I've been awake since."

"Why didn't you wake me?"

"Because you were snoring with your mouth wide open. I didn't wanna bother you."

"Tell me about the bad dream?"

"More like a nightmare." Tamara takes a deep breath and turns toward me. "I've been having it for a while now. I didn't tell you and Ma because I didn't wanna upset you both. And we have enough going on around here."

"That's true, but I still wanna hear it. Why do you think your dream will upset us?"

She trembles. "Because it's about Daddy."

"Then, I definitely wanna know."

"I keep seeing him in the desert. Several clones of him are connected and lined up together spelling the word LOST. I zoom in on all of his faces, and they say disturbing things to me."

"Such as?"

"One says, "I'm sorry" and cries. One says, "I love you girls," and reaches for me. And one says, "I'm not dead." I zoom in on the others and they say stuff like, "Look closely, I'll always be with you, look after each other, and it wasn't supposed to go this way.""

Tears falls across her nose, then onto the bed. I grab a tissue from the box on the dresser, and dab her face.

"How does this dream end?"

Tam sniffles. "Different each time. Sometimes I get close to him, but a sandstorm always separates us like a wall. My side of the wall is hot, sunny, and clear, but he slowly gets covered by the sand and is pulled away. One time I tried sticking my hand through the wall, but it was moving so fast I swear my hands felt a burning sensation when I woke up. Then another time I reached down to pull up one of the clones saying save me, but he melts below the sand before our hands touch."

"Do you mind if I tell Ma all of this?"

"I don't want her to be any sadder than she already is, Van."

"But your dream might help us get closure. Especially Ma. She needs it."

"Fine. You tell her. But don't mention I was crying last night. I don't want her worrying about me."

Tam falls asleep after she tells me her dream. I ease out of the room and pull Ma aside. Her eyes well with tears when I share Tam's dream, but her resiliency won't allow them to fall.

I hold my mother's hand. "I don't know what it means, but it sounds like it could possibly help us learn what happened to him over there."

"You're growing up too fast for me, but I'm proud of the beautiful, caring, intelligent woman you're becoming." She places her palm on my cheek. "Thank you for telling me. I'll make a few calls. But don't you girls worry. I'm the mother. I'll handle it. Okay?"

I nod.

"Let your sister sleep a little while longer. Our dreams can sometimes take everything out of us. Wouldn't you agree?"

"Yes, ma'am." I scowl, wondering how she knows.

"You come help your Aunt Sharon and me in the kitchen for a little while. The faster some of these people get something to eat, the faster they'll leave."

"Gran looks like she's ready for them to leave now."

Ma wraps her arms around me. "Trust me, she is. But the people of her day play their part until the end. It's your generation changing the way things have always been done." She releases me and sighs. "Let's hope that's a good thing."

CHAPTER 29

SALTY SUPERSTITION

Working in the kitchen feels like punishment. Greedy people beg for an extra scoop of grits. Impatient people smack on the bacon before they find a place to sit. Nasty people put their gum on the edge of the plate instead of disposing it in a napkin.

'Thank God for paper plates.'

"Ma, did I do something wrong?" I wipe the dewy formation from my forehead.

"No. Why do you ask?"

"I've been in this kitchen for hours with you and Aunt Sharon. I could use a nap, too."

"We all could use a nap," says Aunt Sharon.

"And why do we have to serve these folks? Especially you and Ma. We are the bereaved."

"Because Mama doesn't want anyone in her kitchen. If you haven't learned that lesson by now, log it in your permanent memory file." Aunt Sharon lectures, then taps the side of my temple. "You don't let anyone in your kitchen. Ever."

"Is this in relation to the reason we're not allowed to eat people's food if we didn't see them cook it?"

"You got it. And if you think this is something, wait 'til after the funeral when Mama makes us clean and comb this house from top to bottom." Ma sighs. "This house is gonna sparkle when this is over."

I mumble under my breath. "I'm not looking forward to that."

Reno and Eileen stroll in with bags from the wholesale store, deli trays, a box of sweet tea fried chicken, and ice. Aunt Sharon takes the bags and places the chicken inside the stove. Ma empties the remainder of items from the grocery bags and Reno taps on the table.

"Hide one of those boxes of salt for me will ya," he says. "The Mrs. was scared all night. *We'en* have no salt to throw on the porch."

"Did y'all put salt down last night?" Eileen asks.

"I didn't, but I will tonight."

"Everybody and their mama was throwing salt around their door when we got home last night. We stopped by two grocery stores when we left here, and they were sold out. I bought the last two I could find this morning."

Aunt Sharon adds, "I stayed at Gina's last night so I didn't have to."

"Have y'all found a dress for the service? I still don't have anything to wear. I'm on my way 'cross the bridge to see what I can find. I'll check the stores over there and grab more salt if they have any. Y'all be easy, and don't let your cousin get too drunk before the wake."

She follows her husband outside, then frees up a space in the driveway.

Aunt Sharon shakes Gran's can of salt. "Good thing she bought extra. Mama's running low herself."

"What's the big deal about salt?" I ask.

"They didn't teach y'all about the ancient white gold in history class?"

"White gold? I don't remember that lesson."

"I swear they're socially promoting *chirren* these days. If they learn anything of value it's at the house." Aunt Sharon scoffs. "At least you read on your own."

"Since she was three. Told me what street I needed to turn on from her car seat." Ma kisses my cheek. "My sweet, smart baby."

"Ah, how lovely. A motherly bragging moment." Aunt Sharon chuckles as she and Ma nudge each other on the elbow. "Baby, salt ain't just for cooking. The first thing you need to know about it, is once upon a time only rich people had the means to buy it. And when I say once upon a time, I mean way, way back in the day when people who looked like us were respected and called Moors."

"I'm familiar with the Moors."

"Well, back in those days, probably ions ago, if you had salt you had money, or gold, which is where the moniker derives— White gold. It was valuable for preserving food back then because of course there weren't any refrigerators or freezers. And it was used as a form of money to trade between countries."

"We did learn about it being used for trade, but hearing it called white gold threw me off."

"There is also black gold AKA black salt. Who better than your Aunt Sharon to teach you about it." Ma tilts her head toward Auntie. "Black gold is popular amongst witches."

"Excuse me?"

"Ain't nothing funny. Witches exist. Even today. They call themselves wiccans. Look it up. And they use black salt to remove hexes and ward off negative energies—But at times they use it to do the opposite."

My brows furrow. "How can it be used both ways?"

"That's a long story and lesson for another time. What's important is where there is good, there is evil. And as time went on people created good and bad reasons for salt overall. It held positive benefits like purifying, storing, and cleaning, but also led to a war. Now here we are today choosing to believe in its purity and ability to provide protection from evil. Have you ever heard anyone say it's bad luck to spill salt?"

"No. But Ma has told me and Tam to take rumors with a grain of salt."

"Well, I'm not talking about that. I'm teaching you why you shouldn't spill it. It's considered bad luck to spill something of such high value, and in doing so, you invite bad luck into your life. Many religions believe this."

"How is it bad to spill it, when y'all are talking about spreading it on the porch? That doesn't make sense."

"Spilling is referring to a careless accident. Intentionally placing white gold or black gold across the threshold of the door is done to protect your space from negativity and evil." Aunt Sharon fans herself. "Whew! The bookworm is making me work today."

She and my mother laugh together as she hides the boxes below the kitchen sink in a plastic bag. My mother opens the box remaining on the table, and carefully fills Gran's salt shaker and the can Aunt Sharon said was near empty.

"There. No salt spilt."

I turn up my lips. "Jeez. Y'all really believe in this superstition after everything we've been through this week?"

Ma and Aunt Sharon stop all movement and turn toward me like robotic Siamese twins. Their eyes stare at me like I cursed in front of them.

"You better believe it, too." Aunt Sharon holds my gaze. "I know a priestess who threw salt on an unwanted presence in her house. She said it shrieked higher than Mariah hitting those octaves in her prime, and it faded before her very eyes."

Ma adds, "If you ever spill salt, take a pinch of it and throw it over your shoulder."

I scratch my head. "Which shoulder?"

"Both."

"No, not both shoulders." Aunt Sharon fusses. "You only toss it over the left shoulder."

"Well I do both shoulders."

"Now I gotta look it up to see which one of us is doing it wrong." She whispers, "I know it's you."

Ma passes me the can of salt as she and Auntie go back and forth on who is wrong, and who is right. "Here, go sprinkle some of this across the door."

Carefully, I pace myself so I don't trip with the newly learned superstition plaguing my every step. I open the door and sprinkle a few beads across the porch.

"Make a line with it across the door!" Aunt Sharon guides me.

I draw a line a few millimeters wide from one edge of the porch to the other, then secure the opening with sweaty, shaky hands and a racing heart. *Whoooo.* The sound catches my attention up above. I look up and nearly blind myself from the sun floating directly above the house.

A rare white owl sits on the lamp post above Granddad's truck in the yard. The blazing sunlight doesn't faze it. It hoots, unbothered by the heat frying everything outside.

My family sitting in front of the big fan are too engaged with one another and miss out on the spectacle. Careful not to scare it away, I call out to them with an exclaimed whisper. They don't hear or see me. But the bird does.

It spreads its wings and hoots again. I stare at it and forget about the can of salt in my hand. My mind wonders if Tamara can understand what it's saying.

I race to Granddad's room to wake her. "What the…" I mutter, when the door swings open.

I jump back, clinging to the can of salt slipping in my sweaty hands as darkness holds my sister hostage. Tears drip from her chin. Pure terror reflects in her eyes. And she sits stiff as a board, too afraid to look away from the volatile black cloud hovering over my favorite chair.

I react so fast it feels like an innate instinct that's been lying dormant. I peel back the top on the salt can and throw wads of salt on the monstrous figure. It shrieks higher than Mariah hitting her highest octave in her prime, flies past Tamara, and jumps into the mirror on the dresser.

I never thought of mirrors as portals, but the mystery behind them, and what I just witnessed has made me a believer. The entity looks back at me, faceless with shiny black eyes moving in a circular motion as it transforms.

Tamara rocks back and forth like a patient in an insane asylum. The black cloud shrieks and Tamara balls into a knot on the bed. I rush to her side as her muffled screams give me goose-bumps. The hair on the back of my neck stands up as I draw a line with the salt at the base of the mirror. Then I wrap my arms around my sister.

She whispers incoherently and softly to herself. I can't make out what she's saying, even though she repeats the same words over and over. Her gibberish frightens me more than the demon hiding in the mirror.

"Ma! Aunt Sharon!" I call, shaking as I comfort my shivering sister's body.

My mother and aunt burst into the room. "What the hell happened in here?!" Ma asks, looking at the line of salt. She rushes over to us and brushes me aside. "What the devil is wrong with you, chile?"

I point to the mirror. "I think the Leprechaun Man can shapeshift. I walked in and found Tam scared stiff from staring at that thing."

"What thing?" they ask.

The son of a bitch had the nerve to disappear like a coward when the adults came into the room. Or was it Aunt Sharon's power and knowledge it ran from? Maybe the salt did the trick? I need to know the answer—In case he reemerges.

"It's gone now, but it resembled the green thing chasing us that night, except it didn't have a body and was in the form of a faceless black cloud. It moved the same, waving back and forth with an unstable face. I threw salt on it and it went inside the mirror."

Aunt Sharon sits next to Tam. "Tam baby, tell us what happened."

Tamara continues to mumble to herself while Ma rocks her in her arms. Aunt Sharon lifts the chain hanging around Tam's neck and cracks a smile. The crystal sparkles like a solo diamond in a mine.

"She was protected. *Thatta* girl keeping your crystal on you. It would help if you could tell us what happened?"

Ma delivers a sharp look at Aunt Sharon. "She's been spooked and is in shock. Give her time. She'll speak when she's ready."

Aunt Sharon walks over to the mirror and studies it. She appears to be looking at her reflection, skimming every inch of the glass from side to side. She raises her hands and presses against the image of herself looking back. In Patois she chants, holding her own gaze as the incantation expels from her lips. Her words bring forth a powerful presence in the room. Low shrieks from the monster echo from the other side of the mirror.

I stand behind Aunt Sharon while Ma covers Tam's ears. Aunt Sharon works her magic, antagonizing the beast. The lights in the room flicker. The shrieks grow faint. Then pure silence. An overwhelming feeling of peace overcomes me. I look at Ma and Tam and they appear to feel the same.

Aunt Sharon exhales sharply. "It won't be coming back in this house."

"What does it want?" I ask.

"I have a theory, but I'd rather be sure before I share it."

Aunt Sharon lies to me. Her response lacks confidence and she is almost always sure of herself, and speaks with conviction and certainty. Ma's eyes narrow at her. She too knows Aunt Sharon is lying, but I keep my assumption to myself. I hope if I wait it out, Ma will do the heavy lifting and see what Auntie is keeping from us.

"We better get back in the kitchen before Mama wonders what's going on in here." Aunt Sharon leaves us behind.

Ma doesn't move an inch. "You go help. We'll come out when your sister is ready."

I'm put back to work against my will. I hold my peace and serve my family and guests lined up around the house for at least an hour until Ma and Tam come back to join us.

Ma looks at all of the people leaning against the wall. "You two go ask your Uncle Wayne to bring in extra folding chairs from the shed."

Tamara walks beside me, rubbing her crystal. We follow Uncle Wayne in the shed and stand back as he sprays bug repellent on a spiderweb guarding the space where the chairs are stacked.

The scent is too much for Tam, so she goes back outside and sits with our cousins under the shade of the big oak tree. I get the feeling she doesn't want to be around me. I wonder if it's because of my inquisitive nature, or my mere presence alone that upsets her.

I follow my instinct and give her some space. I don't ask her to help carry the chairs inside. I leave her alone and do everything Ma asks of me until it's time for Granddad's wake.

The vibrancy of the sky begins to fade. A haze covers its incandescence, but the heat from hell continues to sizzle like an outside sauna.

Both the young and old crowd stand around in the driveway and the grass, waiting for Gran to come out of the house. Chatter fills the yard as the sun begins to set earlier than normal. It's as if the sky forgot what time of day it is. The cerulean blue space above us transitions into indigo, and the stars are suddenly visible. The sky swiftly switches back to pale blue for a millisecond. The glow of the sun flashes from the horizon, then with the snap of a finger returns to its dark path of night.

Collective gasps, sighs and outbursts roar like a packed stadium. "Oh my God! Oh shit! What the!" are shouted the most amongst us.

Uncle Wayne takes off one of Granddaddy's hats he snatched before Uncle Junie claimed it. "What the hell is right?!"

Reno voices, "Now, I ain't never seen the sky do nothing like that in all of my forty-five years!"

Simultaneously, everyone stops talking. The crickets stop chirping. The continuous backdrop of cicadas buzzing also pause. The outside turns completely silent. It's the longest lull I've ever experienced amongst my family.

All of our heads rotate to the sky. We're silenced by the rarity of the unknown phenomenon we all witnessed together. I examine the miles of the dusk colored sky for clues, searching for an object or an angel—Hoping for a glimpse of whatever happened to happen again. To awe us once more.

"That *wasn't no* eclipse," says Uncle Wayne. "It was like God accidentally turned on the day switch then went oops, my bad."

Gran steps out on the porch. "What are all y'all looking at?"

Mumbles and mutters fill the void.

"Somebody better tell me what's going on." She grabs on the rail and wobbles down the stairs. "Cat got everybody's tongue?"

Uncle Junie meets her at the final step. "You had to see with your own eyes, Mama. I'll tell you about it in the car."

<h2>CHAPTER 30</h2>

TREMBLING TEARS

All the talk outside the funeral home is Lizard Man this, Lizard Man that, and questions regarding the sky anomaly. The pianist song of choice creates a somber vibe as we fall in line one by one to march inside the congregation hall.

Granddad's popularity is proven by the number of cars lined up and down the road. The crowd is larger than I expected for a wake. It makes me wonder how many more will show their faces before he becomes one with the dirt.

A distant cousin of his, Pound Cake from Northern Georgia, squeezes in front of me and Tam. She turns around and fast talks us.

"You girls don't mind do you? The humidity is bad down on this end, and my hair is on the verge of sweating out. Y'all are so sweet. Which one of you twins is the oldest?"

Pound Cake sweet talked her cutting ass in line and didn't allow me or Tam to get in a word. Neither one of us corrects her, or answers her stupid question. She knows we aren't twins. And she knew exactly what she was doing when she picked the two of us as her target—To jump in front of everyone else, and to get close to Popcorn and Young Dee standing in front of us.

Tam whispers loud enough for our dear cousin to hear, "Example A—Why Gran is ready for these people to go home."

She glares at us over her shoulder and scoffs. Tam and I snicker while looking at her dead in the eyes. It feels good to share a laugh with my sister. Even better to have her smart mouth back in the midst.

The closer we cross the center of the white boulders on the porch, the quieter the lobby becomes. I quickly miss that silence as the echoes of Gran's cries travel into the hall. It's a sad, agonizing wail that shakes everyone standing between the corridor. Gran is yards ahead of me, but it's clear her loss is stronger than mine, even though we're mourning the same person.

Hearing her cracked voice weep in between sharp breaths every few seconds teaches me a lesson about the bond between a husband and wife. Granddad's death affects us all differently. Compared to the Gran's pain, the rest of the family must feel it with less severity.

Once she is seated, the line begins to flow faster. My chest twists in knots the closer I arrive to view my grandfather's body. Anxiety overwhelms me and I panic. I pass on moving forward and sit down in the aisle seat next to Aunt Zu.

"You alright?" she asks, rocking her baby to sleep.

I nod.

Tamara keeps on, but looks back at me with narrowed eyes. She skims the row for an extra seat, then cuts me with her lashes when she sees the row has filled, and I've left her to view the body alone.

Once the doors of the funeral home have closed, the funeral director, Mr. Swinton, invites family and friends to the front to speak. A mixture of cries and laughs fill the room as stories of Mr. John Sherman in his youth, and in his prime entertain the sadness of his passing away.

Pound Cake takes to the stage and confirms her line jumping ass is indeed a narcissist. Her entire reflection piece focuses more on herself than Granddad.

Tamara looks back at me from the second row up front. We snicker together, shake our heads, and roll our eyes in sync.

Zu peeps us and says, "I hate when people do this." Her head sways side to side. "My God. Hijacking the death of a beloved old man to tell stories about yourself. How sad."

Zu and I giggle the entire time Pound Cake tells what sounds like a made up story she fabricated of the one time Granddaddy visited her side of the family. The very smart Mr. Swinton finally ends her nonsense and interject the moment Pound Cake takes a breath from fibbing to the family.

"That was a lovely share." Mr. Swinton claps his hands. "I'm sure the departed is smiling down from heaven, and would be pleased with your fond memories." He holds out his hand and guides her away from the microphone. "We have one final speaker who has requested to share kind words about Brother Sherman."

The steps of a former classmate tolls the stage. He takes off his hat and places it in front of his chest. He clears his throat and opens with warm words.

"Everyone in this room was lucky to have crossed paths with our brother, John. To know a good-hearted man was to know John. No he wasn't perfect…"

I scanned the room faster than lightning when that man uttered those instigating words.

Zu mumbles, "He better not."

My eyes shift from Gran to Ma, Ma to Aunt Sharon, Aunt Sharon to Uncle Wayne, Uncle Wayne to Uncle Junie, then Uncle Junie back to the speaker. He crafted his next words carefully after receiving the heat and fighting looks from the front row.

"But he was close to it. Always giving, and helping, and donating, and volunteering. A family man who loved his family so, so dearly. I remember the day..."

"Ugh. Here we go. More make this about me stories." Zu sucks her teeth.

"When Junie was born you couldn't tell John he wasn't already father of the year. He was proud to have himself a junior to carry on his name. Always in the barber shop bragging about his baseball games. Talking about his *churn* good grades. How he had to do this and do that to make his family happy. A bright light has dimmed with his passing, but we can't question God and his timing. Let us all be strong at this difficult time, and trust that God will get us through it." The speaker exhales sharply into the microphone for a dramatic effect. "For God is in control."

"Amen!" A voice shouts from the row behind me.

"Amen! Amen!"

Multiple spectators throughout the room ad-lib. Individual claps encourage a few more to join in, then they all clap together. Mr. Swinton shakes the man's hand and shows him off the stage.

Zu moans. "Thank God that's over."

Pastor Moore rises from his seat. He aims for the stage and ignores Mr. Swinton's raised brows and pressed lips.

"This has been a wonderful night of family and friends coming together to spread loving words about our exemplary brother. Hasn't it?" he asks, receiving minimal response. Not to be outdone by the skinny man speaking before him, he continues, "Haven't we been blessed to experience the fellowship and generosity of Brother John in our lifetime. Oh how lucky we are God placed an upstanding gentleman in our lives."

The Amen Corner shouts, encouraging the colorful pastor to carry on with his spiel. He repeats power words from last week's sermon until the elders grunt, and the parishioners slowly trickle out into the hall.

"Now, he knows he ain't supposed to preach tonight," says a woman in front of me.

Zu sighs and places her purse strap over her shoulder. "See you at the house."

The hall fills with praise from the churchgoers who want to worship seven days a week. Pastor Moore calls for members of the choir in attendance to bless us with a song before the dismissal, as if this is Sunday morning and he's in charge.

His flock sings acapella alongside stomps on the hardwood and claps that create a rhythm. They raise their voices and sing until tears surprise me and fall from my eyes.

I'm moved by the vocal powers and the message in the song. I'm moved because my Gran's cries connect with me in a way I can't explain. I feel her pain as well as mine. I feel the loss our family has suffered.

The Pastor moves his hand with a commanding swipe above his head and the choir lowers their voices. The lead singer hums as he speaks.

"Do we have anyone present tonight having a difficult time? I ask that you come to the front right now, and accept God in your heart. It's not Sunday, but there isn't a specific time or day for you to be saved and walk alongside Jesus. Come now and accept his grace and his mercy."

Tamara rises from her seat. She's bawling and shaking. Unrecognizable as the tough, slick-mouthed, girl we all know. Slowly, she steps forward.

Pastor Moore hugs her. "Do we have another one? Is there anyone else present, courageous like this young lady who is ready to walk with the Lord?"

CHAPTER 31
SAVED SOULS

Gran put out notice that no one is to follow us home. She'd had enough of the gathering at her house, the beer cans spilling over in the recycle bin in the backyard, and listening to laughter and gossip when she wanted to lie down in her grief. The over the top display at the wake tipped her over the edge, and she was done with being hospitable while she was in mourning.

The crowd out back shrinks down to one table. The main crew: Uncle Wayne, Popcorn, Cousin Carlos, and Reno keep the noise low to respect Gran's wishes. Ma, Aunt Sharon, Aunt Zu, and Uncle Junie prepare the house for tomorrow. Tamara and I help them for a while, then sneak outside to join the fellas keeping cool in front of the big fan.

"Looks like I'll be having more smoke for myself since my protégé *done went* and got saved on me." Uncle Wayne lights his half-smoked spliff. "What possessed you to do that, girl?"

Tamara shrugs her shoulders. "Y'all don't know what I've been through this week. The things I've seen you wouldn't believe."

Reno guffaws. "Imagine that. A baby who ain't finished hatching all the way *out the egg*, telling us what she's been through."

"She's telling the truth." I co-sign. "Y'all wouldn't understand. Well, Carlos might, but the rest of y'all...Nah."

They all look at each other, then Young Dee says, "We all saw the sky glitch today. We might understand."

Popcorn chimes in. "Tam, do you feel different?"

"No. I didn't feel anything except...Except...Unsure."

"What does that mean?" I ask.

"Did any of you watch what happened while I was up there? Like really watch?"

"You know I did."

Tamara's face scrunches. "Did something seem off to you?"

"Um, the pastor repeated himself twice when he was saving you. I wondered why he did that."

"He was squeezing my head. It was like he was *tryna* make me pass out or something."

Uncle Wayne chuckles. "That man will do anything for attention. I wish you woulda told me that while we were at the wake. I would have stepped to him. I still might."

"I don't think he was doing it to hurt me. I think he wanted me to put on a show or something. You know how people fall over and whatnot when they claim to be touched by the Lord. I got that feeling from him. When I didn't play along, he looked me in my eyes and accepted I wasn't going to play his game, and finally let me go."

Popcorn grunts. "I wondered why he had that disappointed look on his face!"

"So, what I'm hearing is, you got saved by an actor."

"It feels that way." Tamara lowers her head. "Should I have acted a certain way? Shouldn't I feel different?"

"That's a question for your Gran," Reno adds.

The wind whistles and causes a brief silence amongst us. No one admits it, but we're all replaying what took place when Tamara sought spiritual assistance in our heads. Reno kills the silence and cracks open a beer.

He sips the foam loud and sloppy. "I remember when Mrs. Ralph got saved at the church when her husband died. This was way before Pastor Moore was brought in. But hearing you say what he did to you, makes me think about what I always questioned seeing in church when I was a boy. Ya see, Ms. Ralph became a widow in one of the worst ways imaginable. She couldn't get over it. Hell, no one got over it."

I place my hands around the back of my neck as the shrill sound of Reno's voice set the tone of a story I hadn't heard before. He stares off into the darkness with his beer resting in his lap, exhales a deep breath, then continues.

"The short of it is this. Mr. Ralph and his buddies were planning to have a seafood boil at his house. His friends went down to Dead Man Creek to catch crabs while he tended to the yard. Unfortunately, the day didn't go according to plan. He had a freak accident and died cutting the grass. He hit a stump with his lawn mower, flipped over the steering wheel, and well you can guess the rest." Reno's shoulders shiver.

"You're not saying..." Tam asks.

"Yes, that's what I'm saying."

The tabs on cans of beer pop like a popcorn machine in a movie theater. The men in my family guzzle them down with loud gulps in unison around our cypher.

"Is this a true story?" I ask.

"I wouldn't make something like that up."

I stutter. "The—lawn—mower—chopped—that—man up?"

"Yes. I was trying not to say it."

I hold my chest. "Sorry...I just find that horrible, and unbelievable. My God."

"It was beyond horrible. That's why Mrs. Ralph couldn't get over it. Well that—And what happened next."

Carlos finishes off his can. "How can this get any worse?"

"Well, on the side of the house where he was killed, a shadow formed. It didn't matter what time of day it was, a permanent shadow casted on their house, and y'all know the sun has to be in a certain position for a shadow to be visible. Right?"

We all nod.

"Well, Mrs. Ralph of course wanted to sell the house, but word had traveled about the shadow. Nobody was buying a house where a man died the way he did, or a house with a spirit shadow. So, Mrs. Ralph asked my daddy and some other men to come by the house and paint the outside to get rid of the shadow. Daddy said they painted the entire house, the porch, the bricks, even the shudders, but no one wanted to paint that side of the house. Mrs. Ralph was happy with the new look, until she came outside and saw that the side was still light yellow with the shadow haunting her. Daddy said the look on her face was heartbreaking, so he took it upon himself and cast the first stroke of paint on the vinyl, proving to the other men, nothing was gonna happen to them. They all pitched in and painted that side quickly to put a smile on Mrs. Ralph's face. It lasted all but two minutes. The shadow came right back."

Popcorn stands up. "Damn! So what did she do?"

"There wasn't anything she could do. The shadow became a permanent fixture on the house, and no one would buy it. Then, one day she came to the front for altar call and asked for extra prayer, and to be resaved. This is the part I always think of. One of the men standing up there started dancing and carrying on and shaking about after the preacher touched his forehead. Then this lady who was always regal and proper came up there to supposedly calm the man down, but then she started shaking all about. But what got me was what I saw with my own two eyes.

That prim and proper lady purposely took out the pins in her hair so she could shake it. I remember wondering, *'Why would she do that? Why couldn't she catch the holy ghost without shaking her hair for show? This is all fake.'* Then, the pastor touched Mrs. Ralph's forehead with his index finger." He points to Tamara. "She had the same look you had on your face tonight."

"She probably didn't wanna put on a show. Same as me."

"Exactly. Ever since then, I've always been skeptical of people who pretend that they are closer to God than the rest of us, and I serve in my own private way." He takes a swig. "And I'm saying this to you because I want you to know it didn't take going up there for the change you are looking for. Just pray."

Reno pats the back of Tamara's hand. A tear strolls down her cheek and she nods in agreement.

"What happened to Mrs. Ralph?" I ask.

"She eventually got rid of the shadow and the house."

Tamara's eyes light up with joy. "Because of the prayers?"

"Perhaps. It's hard to say. A few weeks after she went up for altar call, a man by the name of Larry Dutch started sniffing around with the intent to spend her money. Ya see people 'round here talk too much, and someone at the bank spread how much money Mrs. Ralph deposited from the accidental insurance. Larry worked his way into her good graces and started keeping up her yard. One day he took it upon himself to call in some excavators to remove the stump that killed Mr. Ralph. The workers caused quite a commotion once it was removed. It was rumored that as soon as they lifted it from the ground, the shadow on the side of the house faded. And below the stump was a million dollars in cash, coins, and jewels buried in a wooden box."

Carlos throws his can toward the bin. "Get the hell *outta* here!"

"*I'ne* lying. When that shadow disappeared, the world

opened up for old Mrs. Ralph. She finally sold her house and got the hell on from 'round here."

Uncle Wayne chuckles. "She cashed in big time and left town so fast, Larry blinked and found himself back at the check and go."

Reno joins in with an amused laugh. "So what I'm saying is —Prayer works."

CHAPTER 32

TAMARA'S TRUTH

Ma comes into the room to check on us before bed.

"Today was more eventful than I thought it would be. Are you girls alright?"

"Yes, ma'am." I answer for the both of us.

"Tam? You okay? Anything you need to talk about?"

"Yeah, but I'm saving it for Gran."

"Why not me?"

"No offense, she's more experienced with what I need." Tam turns her back to Ma.

"Okay, I guess. As long as you talk to one of us, I suppose it's fine."

Ma's face is frowned when she shuts the door. Her voice doesn't sound as strong as it normally does, and Tam choosing to seek counsel from Gran instead of her makes me feel bad for her. I keep that in mind when I wrestle to fall asleep.

My constant wiggling for a sweet spot disturbs Tam.

"Did you see anything peculiar on our way home tonight?" she asks.

"No. But I wasn't paying attention to the road. Did you see something?"

"I thought I saw something glowing in the middle of the road, but none of you said anything so I kept quiet. And when we passed the mark, I looked back and whatever it was stood up with an even brighter light in its hand, then ascended into the sky. It was probably nothing but my mind playing tricks on me after everything that happened today."

"Today was crazy, innit?"

"Crazy is an understatement."

"Are you sure you're alright?"

"I think so." Tam turns around to face me.. "What about you?"

I scowl at her. "What about me?"

"Why didn't you view the body?"

I pause. With everything the two of us have been through, I'm not sure I can explain my travel to the other side without sounding as if I'm exaggerating. I don't doubt that she will believe me. I doubt my ability to explain the experience correctly.

Finally, I bite the bullet and water down my response. "I didn't like how Granddaddy looked the last time I saw him. I couldn't put myself through seeing him like that again."

"You mean the night when…"

I cut her off. "Yeah, that night," I lie. "Did you honestly feel getting saved would rescue you from being one of the touched?"

"Yes. I don't want these inherited abilities. I wanna be normal."

"Instead of extraordinary?"

"You heard me. Good night."

Tam turned her back to me. Before she falls asleep I tell her.

"Be easy on Ma. She's holding herself together for our sake. Whatever you wanna talk to Gran about, you should tell her, too. Good night."

I count how many rectangles I can form from the cutouts in the vent on the ceiling. Sometime later, I drift off and find myself in the darkness with muffled voices behind me.

Slowly, I walk towards them with my fists balled, but I'm not scared. A feeling of need covers me as my steps move forward toward a voice I felt deeply connected to. I'm in a dream world—Tam's dream world, or more like her nightmare.

Our close bond has drawn me inside her reverie for a reason. I'm back in my grandfather's room, standing in the doorway watching a replay of the moment Tamara came face to face with the apparition that startled her.

This time I notice she doesn't blink. Her eyes never look at me when I burst into the room. They remain fixated on the black cloudy figure speaking in a coarse, calm, commanding tone.

"You know who I am, don't you?" It says.

Tamara looks on in horror. She's catatonic and entranced. Fear has crippled her. A dark one seeks her in a house of God. A house built on prayer and obedience to the light.

"I am Death, and I can take you when I please. You've figured that much out, haven't you?"

Tamara speaks, barely moving her lips. "Not in this house you won't," she mutters. "This is a God fearing house. You have no weight here."

"False! As you can see I am welcomed here...Thanks to you." It chitters.

"I don't follow," she grits through her teeth.

"Your heart brought me here. It is you who helps me linger. That jealousy you carry around for the sister who loves you dearly led me your way. If only she knew how you truly felt about her." It hisses, forming a face then waves to erase it.

"I love my sister."

"Do you? Is jealousy love? Is envy love?"

Tamara's hands rise and clasp in prayer pose. "God, I call

upon you to remove this devil out of this house and stay away from me."

"I'm no devil. The devil lives in humans, like yourself. People like you welcome him in and do his dirty work, then you're delivered to me."

I witness the first tear fall from Tamara's face as she repeats her prayer request to God, then I move forward into the room. This is when I toss salt on the demon, but the jar is missing from my hands.

I sigh. *'This is Tam's recollection, not my own.'*

The cloud shrieks as I get closer. It rises and hovers over the chair and forms a menacing face to stare at me. My fingers tut in a somatic form I'm unfamiliar with. It comes to me naturally and on time as it scares the frightening figure into the mirror.

It looks back at Tamara. "Until you call upon me." It screeches and fades away.

Tamara turns to me and bursts into a silent cry. I keep watch on the mirror as I ease my way to console her quivering body. She gasps and her voice becomes audible. It becomes clear what she was repeating when I found her in real time was the prayer she recited, ""God, I call upon you to remove this devil out of this house and stay away from me.""

I listen to her mumble it over and over, still watching the mirror closely. When the cloud who called itself Death doesn't return, I muster the courage to ask my sister a question I never thought possible.

"Is it true, Tam? You hate me?"

"How are you here?" she murmurs.

The figure reappears in the mirror and stares at me with cold, glowing yellow eyes. "Tell her, my girl." It shifts its cloudy face into the green one that Ma shot at. It grins at me, then morphs back into a murky haze.

Rage begins to grow inside of me. "Are we not as close as I think?" I brush Tam's shoulders.

"We are." She inhales. "Don't listen to that thing."

"How can I not? He admitted your ill will feelings for me has given him purpose to harbor inside of you."

"And I'm still here." It croons, easing through the glass.

I shock it with a swift zap of fire, piercing it back inside.

'Damn, I need the jar of salt to trap him. But this isn't my dream.'

"She lies, you know." It trills, waving in an unsteady motion.

"Why would you envy me, Tam? You're my sister. I love you. Make this thing go away."

"I've been trying. Why do you think I got saved today?"

Finally, the truth spills from my sister's mouth. I would have never guessed she felt anguish towards me with her perfect pretending. I'm also saddened to learn she's been wearing a mask to cover her hate for so long. But I still love her, and will protect her with my own life.

"What did I do to make you feel this way about me?"

She sniffles. "I don't hate you, Vanya. Sometimes I just feel slighted in your presence. I'm the oldest, yet I walk in your shadow because of how smart and brave you are."

"You're just as smart as me. And I think you've proven you are brave today. You faced this thing." I throw a flame ball at the mirror. "You heard a cat speak, and you may have given us hope to find Daddy with your vision. Your gift is not allowing you to walk away from it. More importantly, you and Ma have something in common. I'd say you have more than enough reasons not to feel the way you do about me."

"What about all of the boys that like you?"

I scowl. "Ricky is one boy."

'Where is she going with this?'

"He's not the only one. I never told you Marlon Keys asked to walk me home one day when you had track practice. I never felt so seen before. He carried my bookbag, flaunted his million dollar smile at me, and I thought we had chemistry until he asked for our number—To call you."

My mouth drops open. "What? Why didn't you tell me this?"

"Because I felt like a fool flirting with him, and thinking this cute boy likes me, only to come second to you yet again."

"Yet again? You don't mean you like Ricky, too?"

The apparition laughs villainously in the mirror once Tamara breaks our gaze. I peek at it with a side eye, then wait for Tamara to look in my direction again.

"I didn't know you liked Ricky."

"I liked Saul. That situation with him really did a number on me."

"You didn't like Saul. That was some sort of glamour magic he used on you. He was probably sent by that thing." I throw more fire at the mirror. "I'm just glad you got away from him before you got in too deep."

"I feel stu…"

"You were vulnerable and we all make mistakes. But I hope you know I would choose you over any boy. You are my sister. And you'll always come first."

The sprite figure laughs at us. "She wouldn't choose you."

I grow irritated with the troublemaker lingering and instigating discord between us.

"I'm here," a voice whispers in my ear.

I look over my shoulder. Great Great Great Gran is here. I'm over the moon to see her here. Her presence comforts me and gives me strength as she proves that I don't have to fight my battles alone.

I point to Tamara. "It's her dream," I tell her.

"Time to get rid of it and wake her up."

I face the menacing cloud and bolt a continuous flame at it through the mirror. It screams and shrieks encircled in the fire.

"I'll be watching! I'll be watching!" It threatens, until the dresser burns to the ground.

Great Great Great Gran opens her mouth and aims a stream of water on the flames. She drowns what's left of the demon until he fades away into a ghostlike figure, then disappears. She raises her hands and water sprinkles from her fingers to eliminate the smoke. She smiles at us and vanishes in the realm. She doesn't say goodbye. There's no need because she'll always be there.

"Now would be a good time to wake up," I say to Tamara.

"*Huugh!*" Tamara gasps, and sits up on the bed.

We're back in our bedroom. Our house. Our reality. We embrace, both dripping wet with sweat. Her heart races with intensity, beating like drums that I can feel from simply touching her back.

"I love you, Tam."

"I'm sorry, Van. I love you, too." She squeezes me so tight, I believe her.

The rooster from The Perrin Farm down the street crows. We unlock our arms and turn toward the window. The moon has hours left on its shift as the break of dawn slowly approaches.

"It's too early for that hen to be going off. What do you think it sees?" I ask.

Tamara looks at me with tired eyes. "It's no telling this time of night."

CHAPTER 33

GOD'S GRACE

There is no going back to sleep for us. Tam and I talk until the sun begins to heat our side of the house. We discuss everything under the sun except for our family magic: boys, lost friendships, teachers that treated us unfairly, our uncles' beef, secret crushes, and fears to overcome.

We bond over what boys are the cutest and coolest, how to convince Gran to get rid of the dresser in Granddaddy's room, the weirdness of people calling us stair-step twins, and if we'll continue our legacy with children after listening to Zu's baby cry as loud as the rooster.

Ma blasts her classic jazz albums to drown out the noise. We lie back and listen to the tunes, sluggish and tired from the fight we endured overnight. An hour later, she slings pots and pans and fills the house with mouthwatering aromas of cheese eggs, buttery biscuits, and brown sugar bacon.

I rub my stomach. "She's pulling out all the stops today."

"It has to be her way of grieving. I haven't seen her or Aunt Sharon cry yet. Maybe a tear or two, but not like how Gran cried yesterday."

"It's possible they have when they're alone. There's more than one way to grieve. "

"True."

Ma knocks on the door. Her eyes are puffy and stretched wide. She has many reasons to cry. To be sad. To not look like herself at the moment. But her tired eyes reflect more than grief and sadness in my opinion. They carry the burden of insight and premonition, and the pain of not having the answer she seeks the most.

"Y'all get up and get dressed. Long day ahead of us."

"Ma, you okay?" I groan.

"Why are you making that noise? You've got a long time before you know what it feels like to be tired at the beginning of the day."

"We didn't sleep last night."

"Neither did I. I can't believe I'm burying my father today. Let alone everything else that's happened this week. Then, The Perrin's mangy rooster cock-a-doodled all night long."

"That's what kept us up."

Ma scoffs. "I wondered all night what ruffled its feathers. Probably a tomcat."

"I wondered if it was the Lizard Man? Did we put salt on the porch last night?" Tam adds.

Ma and I turn to Tamara as a prolonged silence shifts the tone of the room.

"Okay. Enough of that. Get dressed and come eat. We should be heading over to Mama's shortly."

The vibe feels different at Gran's house this morning. We walk into a calm house. The radio isn't playing chilling hymns with a choir humming in a monotonous tone. It's extremely quiet unlike it's been for the past few days—Similar to the mornings before Sunday service.

As I pass the big window in the foyer, I notice the biggest difference. Granddad isn't hacking away in his room from sneaking in a smoke. He swore his suction ashtray hid the smell of his long, brown cigarettes Gran forbade him to smoke in the house.

The smell of coffee isn't brewing, and the television isn't blasting the national reverend preaching to a flock of white folks poised for the camera. And here we are dressed in our Sunday's best, but it's not Sunday, and a big part of the family is missing.

Random people drop off food, but they leave this time. No lingering or loitering. No fighting for a place to sit in the house. The day of the funeral spares us the drama of visitors because they too have to get ready to meet us at the church. It's odd how peaceful the day of the main event is.

Carlos and Reno direct the family cars where to park. Ma and Aunt Sharon help Gran get dressed, then sit at her side in the living room until it's time to leave. They whisper when they speak. And when their mouths are closed, they talk with their eyes.

Uncle Wayne and Uncle Junie meet with Mr. Swinton outside and dictate who will ride in the family cars provided by the funeral home. I look past them at the parade of family and friends parked down the road so far, it's impossible to see where they end.

Mr. Swinton heads toward the house. I push Tamara into the hallway outside of Granddaddy's room. She elbows me and complains.

"What are you doing?"

Mr. Swinton announces, "It's time."

Ma and Aunt Sharon assist Gran to her feet. They pass her to Mr. Swinton and she grabs her pocketbook with a tight grip.

"We don't have much time. Stop acting like you're not curious to see it for yourself." I sigh, opening the door. "Just as I thought."

Tamara pokes her head inside.

I run my fingers across the wood. "It's warm to the touch."

She enters the room and slowly places her fingertips on it, then quickly pulls them away. "We have to convince Gran to get rid of this thing."

I nod, as a tap on the window steals our attention. The cat from the tree sits upright on its paws and stares at us with a tricky smile on its face.

"You think that thing can shift into a cat?" Tam mumbles.

"I don't know, but that smile is disturbing. Is it saying anything? Can you read its mind?"

"I'm not picking up on anything."

"Girls!" Ma yells from the front room.

We jump at the sound of Ma's voice, looked at each other, then back to the window. The cat winks and hops down from the sill. Tamara's shoulders lock in place. Her face turns to stone as she takes several sharp breaths.

I place my arm around her shoulders and lead her from the room. "Maybe it wants to be friends," I say, and close the door behind us.

The sun shines bright, instantly boiling us as we march down the steps of the porch. We blend with the members of our family already lined up to ride inside the town cars and limousines. Uncle Wayne and Uncle Junie escort Gran outside. She walks between the parallel lines we've formed with her head bowed and face hidden behind black lace and a fancy hat.

A sudden drizzle begins to fall from the sky while the sun continues to cook us. The majority of women shield their pressed tresses with fans and purses. A few men use their jackets as umbrellas, but no one leaves the formation during Gran's stroll.

Zu bounces her baby. "They say when it does this, the devil is beating his wife."

Eileen shushes her. "*I'ne* never heard that one."

Aunt Sharon whispers to Ma. "Mama is doing this."

Ma nods. "I know."

I turn toward Gran standing hand in hand with my uncles. Her cry isn't ear scratching like last night. It's silent, yet still infectious.

The clasp on purses unfasten, and the rustling of tissues wipe every sensitive eye and sympathetic person that is present. The delicate shower follows us to the church, then suddenly stops when Gran wipes her teary face and exits the car.

Outside, the choir can be heard rejoicing. Inside, their heads sway side to side as they serenade us with a mid-tempo hymn during our walk down the aisle.

Tam pulls on my arm. "Don't do what you did yesterday."

"I promise I won't. I want to see him one final time."

It's strange accepting Granddaddy is really gone. After all of the drama, family, and friends I've encountered following his death, it feels real today with the ambiance of sadness coated in black throughout the church.

I'm pleased to see he is no longer gray. Color has been restored to his physical, and his face resembles what I imagine peace looks like, or when a soul has been set free.

I touch his head and cradle his cold hand one final time. "You're missed, Cool Man," I whisper, then follow Tam to our seats next to Ma and Aunt Sharon sobbing hard in the front row.

The doors of the church creak shut when the ushers line up in doubles in front of the altar. Mr. Swinton's footsteps silences the hall when he approaches the altar. He stands in the front of the church and begins the home going service. I tune out after a few words and my eyes wander around the church.

The feeling of prayer covers me, and I silently talk with God. I

ask him to remove all unwelcomed spirits and unexplained enti-
ties. To protect my family from evil, harm, and danger. To shield
my family from the old wives tale that death comes in threes.

Mr. Swinton nods to Gran and places his hand on the lid
above Granddaddy's head. A low wail escapes Gran's mouth. My
uncles hold her in their arms as the clasp locks in place, and frees
our beloved John Sherman to the other side.

Casket closed.

AFTERWORD

Special Acknowledgment to Miakai E. Robinson

Never stop making us laugh 🩶

REVIEWS ENCOURAGE VORACIOUS INTEREST EVERY WHERE TO SUPPORT

ME, THE AUTHOR

I GREATLY APPRECIATE IT

XOXO

THANK YOU
FOR READING
LOWCOUNTRY LEGENDS!

We would love it if you'd leave a review. Thanks!

Acknowledgments

THANK YOU! To the following people for supporting this story, encouraging me to keep writing, proofreading, editing, and sharing it with their family and friends. I appreciate you!

Mia Lindler
Monica Singletary
Ashley Outing
Kelley Wilson
Markeshia Kirksey
Keedra Norris
Shawn Robinson
Michael Brice Lampkin
The Kochems Family
The Taylor Family
Hubert Wicker
Larry Robinson
Kimani Lauren

T.K. RICHARDS is a multi-genre author with novels and novellas in romance featuring Black Romance, Interracial/Multicultural Romance & Paranormal Romance, Speculative Fiction, Women's Fiction, and Domestic & Suspense Thrillers.

As a graduate of Limestone University, T.K. has honors in Expository Writing, & was the Poet Laureate of her graduating class. When she is not writing, she is immersed in the world of tennis, baking, and binge watching movies—mostly comedy as she loves to laugh.

For more information about **T.K. Richards**, visit www.tkrichards.com and subscribe to her newsletter at: https://tkrichardsnewsletter.ck.page Follow **T.K. RICHARDS** here:

instagram.com/t.k.richards

pinterest.com/TKWrites

tiktok.com/@tkrwrites

youtube.com/tkrichards

goodreads.com/T.k.richards

bookbub.com/authors/t-k-richards

amazon.com/author/Tkrichards

patreon.com/tkrichards

tkrichards.substack.com